"Get down."

Mallory tackled her son, Maverick, behind the mound and slid her gun from her waistband. Sawyer hit the ground beside her. The shot seemed to come from the east line of trees. "Do you see him?"

"No." Sawyer looked over the mound, and a gunshot kicked up dirt between them.

Maverick huddled in a ball at her knee, and her heart went out to him. She glanced at Sawyer.

"We need to take cover."

"I'm calling for backup." He quickly texted someone. "I can cover you while you make for the barn."

"I can't risk Maverick getting hurt."

"I agree. That guy's gun is more powerful than ours, and he has the protection of the trees."

A hooded man with a rifle sprinted closer, behind a tall oak tree. He looked to be the same guy from last night.

She fired a shot, but her target was already in position. She looked over her shoulder. Her daddy's old Ford tractor with the cab sat behind them.

Sawyer saw what she was looking at. "Go."

"Stay with me, Mav." She pointed. "We're going to get in that tractor..."

Connie Queen has spent her life in Texas, where she met and married her high school sweetheart. Together they've raised eight children and are enjoying their grandchildren. Today, as an empty nester, Connie lives with her husband and her Great Dane, Nash, and is working on her next suspense novel.

Books by Connie Queen

Love Inspired Suspense

Justice Undercover
Texas Christmas Revenge
Canyon Survival
Abduction Cold Case
Tracking the Tiny Target
Rescuing the Stolen Child
Wilderness Witness Survival
Searching for Justice

Thunder Ridge Justice

Shielded by the Cowboy
Texas Cowboy Protector

Visit the Author Profile page at LoveInspired.com.

TEXAS COWBOY PROTECTOR

CONNIE QUEEN

Recycling programs for this product may not exist in your area.

ISBN-13: 978-1-335-95777-1

Texas Cowboy Protector

For questions and comments about the quality of this book, please contact us at CustomerService@Harlequin.com.

Love Inspired
22 Adelaide St. West, 41st Floor
Toronto, Ontario M5H 4E3, Canada
www.LoveInspired.com

HarperCollins Publishers
Macken House, 39/40 Mayor Street Upper,
Dublin 1, D01 C9W8, Ireland
www.HarperCollins.com

Printed in Lithuania

Knowing this, that the trying of your faith worketh
patience. But let patience have her perfect work,
that ye may be perfect and entire, wanting nothing.
—*James* 1:3–4

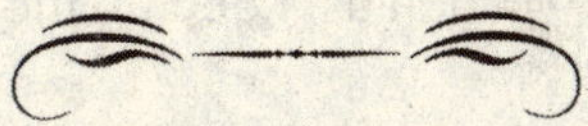

I would like to dedicate this book to my daughters-in-law: Susana, Olga, Krista and Sneha. I see you work hard to help take care of the house, kids and my sons. I'm indeed blessed for all of you to be a part of our family and couldn't wish better for my grandkids. Keep up the good work!

ONE

The rain came down in a sudden burst, making Mallory Foster's windshield wipers squeak in protest. The rubber on the driver's side wiper had come loose, causing it to move in sporadic jumps. She let off the accelerator of her Jeep Wrangler, hoping to avoid giant potholes. Visibility was almost zilch, but she knew the area like the back of her hand. Or at least she used to.

A check to her rearview mirror showed nothing but rivers of droplets on her back window. A few miles back, a vehicle appeared to be following her since she turned off the main highway, then a mile or so back, it'd disappeared. Had they been following her since she left Country Corner? Whether they turned onto another road or simply turned off their headlights, she didn't know.

The pouring rain continued to fall from the night skies. The mood was perfect for her homecoming. It'd been five years since she'd stepped foot on her parents' ranch. Five years since her brother, Sam, was suspected of murdering three people. Five years since Sam was killed in a high-speed chase while running from the Cedar Hollow police.

Her mom died within a month of alcohol poisoning after Sam's death, and her dad remarried and moved to Florida months later. The townspeople of Cedar Hollow, Texas, had turned their backs on her family, treating them like every member was responsible for the three deaths.

Mallory didn't believe Sam was guilty, but rather, he was framed. He'd made some bad decisions when he was younger, like stealing from a neighbor when he was a teenager, but he'd been making strides to get and keep his life straight. The night of the murders, he'd been driving on a dangerous road with sharp curves, and his truck was found in the bottom of a steep ravine. Sam was knocked unconscious. The length of the brake marks on the road before impact proved he had been speeding—something he'd done often. The police discovered three dead bodies, all residents of Cedar Hollow, two with gunshot wounds in the back seat of his pickup. They found a gun and one of the victims' broken jewelry in the console of Sam's Nissan Titan. Ballistics proved the gun was the murder weapon. It's not that she could blame investigators, because the evidence was strong, but the Cedar Hollow Police was small with less than ten employees. Chief Trevett had only been at the department for seven months and hadn't wanted to call in outside help, except for the use of the county's lab facilities. Two days later, when the police went to arrest him, Sam tried to evade them. In a high-speed chase, Sam's truck was hit by a train, and he was killed instantly. Mallory wanted the police to keep investigating because her brother had no previous connections with the victims. But they believed Sam had broken into the house to burglarize it, surprised the owners who were home, and in a panic, he killed them.

If Sam had come to her instead of running, everything could've ended differently. She could only assume he ran because he had been afraid of going to jail with the evidence piling against him.

The situation put her at enmity with the one person she thought would stand by her side. Sawyer Cantrell. After dating for over a year while working as Texas State Troopers together, they got engaged to be married, but all that changed when he gave up on Sam's innocence, believing the evidence pointed against her brother. One of the victims was Phillip Pennington, a good friend of Sawyer. Deep down, she believed this pitted Sawyer against Sam. Mallory felt abandoned by the one person she should be able to depend on. She broke the engagement and took a state trooper job in the panhandle of West Texas. Four years later, she finally got her break and became a Texas Ranger.

Mallory intended to clear her brother's name, now that the badge of the Texas Rangers gave her the resources to get answers to her questions. She had created social media pages about the case, seeking information from the public. Throughout the years, except for a few people offering condolences and offering up prayers, most people commented that Sam had received his just reward by getting hit by a train. A few even lectured Mallory for setting up the pages and not letting the victims' families grieve in peace.

A month ago, someone anonymously contacted her by email saying they'd heard someone had bragged about owning the gun that had killed Phillip Pennington, Phillip's sister Tilda and their friend Wilson Newport. However, the gun was supposed to be in the evidence room at the police station.

After Mallory's lieutenant gave her permission to look into the case, she'd also noticed one of the neighbors had witnessed a dark sports car parked in front of Tilda's home at the time of the murders. Investigators never learned the owner of the car. Also, there were fingerprints on the steering wheel that didn't match Sam or the victims. Most of the people in Cedar Hollow were good and law-abiding, but they had been wrong about Sam. They had been wrong to turn their backs on her parents and Mallory.

If she must fight alone, then so be it. Her life had been derailed, and no matter what she did, she couldn't find her footing again.

The old farmhouse appeared cold and run-down—neglected. The fields that used to have golden wheat and green pastures for cattle, now stood overgrown with temporary muddy rivers running amok.

Welcome home, Mallory Foster.

"Mom, are we at Grandma's and Papa's yet?"

Mallory smiled and turned to her four-year-old son, Maverick, as he rubbed the sleep from his eyes and sat up in his seat. She rubbed the top of his head. "Yes, we are, sleepyhead."

"Oh." He pressed his nose against the window like his first glimpse of the old farm was something to behold.

As she pulled to a stop, she noticed the house was shrouded in darkness. She had called the electric company yesterday to have it turned back on since Mrs. Lansbury, the woman who'd rented the place not long after Mallory's dad moved to Florida, had moved out three months ago. Mallory grabbed her flashlight from the console. "Stay right here. Let Mom make sure the electricity is on."

"Okay," Maverick said.

Even though it was May, the storm had brought cooler weather and he left the engine running with the heat on. She climbed out the driver's side, and a blast of cold rain sent chills to her core. She ran to the front porch, dodging puddles as best as she could.

Thunder rumbled, giving her the creeps. She fumbled with the key and swung the front door wide just in case someone was waiting for her. No one should be here, but years of working as a Texas State Trooper and, as of last year, the Texas Rangers had taught her to expect the unexpected. For two seconds, she hesitated in the open doorway.

Keeping the house keys in her hand, she flipped up the light switch. The house remained dark. "Great."

She clicked on the flashlight as something skittered across the floor in another room.

The storm raged on. Had the electric company not turned on her electricity or had the storm made it go out? Many times, when she was a child and the lights went out, her dad would look across to the closest neighbor's farm, to see if their security light had gone out. If so, the power would have probably gone out.

She glanced out of the large living room window.

The old mimosa tree's branches danced in the wind. Even as a kid, she'd thought the tree was scary looking at night.

Lightning lit up the sky, and a half second later, a huge boom shook the ground. Poor Maverick. He was probably nervous of the storm.

A door slammed somewhere in the house, making her jump. She was certain it was just the draft of her opening the front door making it slam, but she wanted to perform a walk-through of the house anyway.

She moved through the house, careful not to be close to the windows. Most of Mrs. Lansbury's things were gone from when she moved into a nearby town. She claimed the farm had too much upkeep and was too lonely. A broken recliner sat in the far corner, and a few pictures hung on the wall.

She walked back to her parents' empty bedroom. Sadness filled her. Next, she walked past her old bedroom to

Sam's. A glance in the dark room showed Sam's bed was just like he left it. Mrs. Lansbury had no need for the extra bedroom. A photo of him graduating high school still sat on his dresser.

Something reflected again, and she stepped to the window. A shadow moved across the yard. The rain had slowed, and the lightning was now in the east.

She hurried down the stairs.

The front door swung open, making her jump and pull her service weapon. "Maverick." She dropped her gun to her side, relieved it was him and not someone who was lurking around. "Mama told you not to get out of the Jeep. You need to listen to me."

She quickly shut the door to keep the rain from blowing in.

He cocked his head at her. "Who was that man, Mommy?"

Her heart skipped a beat. "What do you mean?"

His little hand pointed at the front door. "That man."

Chills skittered down her spine as she looked up to see a person in a hoodie jog by the front window.

"Stay here." She turned the knob, planning to ask the man what he was doing on her property.

Boom!

She tackled Maverick to the living room floor, wrapping her arms around his body to protect him as a piece of burning metal smashed the window and landed against her arm. Reflexively, she jerked her arm free and scooted back. Flames eerily showed through glass shards.

"Ma-ma!" Maverick screamed and clawed at her, trying to get closer.

"It's okay. I've got you." Where did the man go? She kept her grip on Maverick as she climbed to her feet, put him on her hip and hurried for the cover of the wall. She glanced out the east window. It looked like a man was standing underneath a tree to the far side of the yard, but she couldn't be certain.

Another loud bang sounded as an additional explosion came from her Jeep. That could've been the gas tank. Had it been caused by gunfire?

With Maverick to protect, she couldn't run after the man to apprehend him. Instead, she moved to the old brick counter in the kitchen and knelt on the floor. She moved Maverick into the place where they used to keep the trash can because it was totally surrounded with brick and would be the safest place for him if the man fired on them. She sat beside him. With one arm around her son, she said. "We're going to stay right here and call for help."

She dialed 9-1-1 and quickly explained to the dispatcher she'd had an intruder who blew up her vehicle and gave her the address. After Mallory assured her neither of them were injured, the operator told her a deputy and the fire department were on the way.

She wanted to see if the person was still out there. The last thing she needed was someone coming through the back door or shooting at her if she walked by a window. "Stay here. Do not move. Mama's going to make certain the man is gone, but it's important you listen to me."

He nodded. "Okay. I listen."

"Love you." She kissed him on top of the head.

As soon as she was on her feet, she hunched over, staying low, and moved to the wall. Thankfully, she shouldn't be easily seen with it being dark in the house, and she was wearing her navy jacket. She peeked through the edge of the window.

Wood splintered by her cheek a fraction before the single gunshot sounded. She returned a couple of shots.

The intruder was still there. A glance back at Maverick showed his eyes were wide with fear.

Why was this happening? She had no answer except it must be because someone wanted to stop her from investigating the murders. How did someone already know she was back in Cedar Hollow to clear her brother's name?

As he was on his way home from a late night after dropping off two saddles with the saddler in another county, Sawyer Cantrell thought he heard a gunshot. With the thunderstorm lingering, he figured it was thunder. When an orange glow showed on the horizon, he decided to check it before he went home to the ranch.

It wasn't unheard of that a lightning strike would cause a fire. He turned his truck off the rural highway onto a dirt road. His tires kicked up mud, making it hit the side of this truck and even the side windows. He hoped he didn't get stuck. After a long day, that would be all he needed. His truck was four-wheel drive, but still. No one hardly used this road, and the county did little maintenance on it when so many others had more traffic.

The only properties back here were the old Foster home, and a piece of pastureland that Felix Chad leased for his cattle from another property owner. The rest were pine forests that were only used during hunting season, if then. As he drew closer, he realized something was on fire at the Foster home. Was the house on fire? If so, fire trucks would never reach the location before it burned to the ground.

He hit the gas harder.

Even though it'd been years since he'd been here, it still

felt like yesterday he used to drive over on a regular basis to see Mallory. He pulled into the drive.

The house had not caught fire, but a vehicle that sat in front of it was engulfed in flames. Who would be here, especially this time of night? Last he'd heard, Mrs. Lansbury had moved out. He stopped his truck several yards back so the embers wouldn't land on it and hurried toward the driver's side of the vehicle.

He realized it was a yellow Jeep Wrangler. He looked into the red-hot flames but didn't see anyone inside. Just to be certain no one was in the burning vehicle, he hurried to the passenger side. The flames licked up too high to get close. It looked like a child's car seat inside.

He prayed there wasn't a child inside.

"Texas Ranger. Move away from the vehicle."

Sawyer spun toward the voice. A person stood in the shadows of the front porch of the home and pointed a gun at him.

He lifted his hands into the air and took a step back. It only took a second to realize by the curves that it was a woman who aimed the weapon. "I heard an explosion. I was just seeing if anyone needed help."

"Sawyer. Is that you?" The voice sounded dismayed.

"Mallory Foster?" He squinted. Sure enough, that was her standing there in her jeans, navy jacket and boots. Her damp blond hair hung almost to her shoulders. She was the last person he'd expected to be here. "You can put the gun down."

She dropped the weapon to her side and glanced back over her shoulder into the house before returning her attention to him. "Step inside." She nodded toward the house. "Someone paid us a visit, complete with an arsenal welcome."

He followed her into the dark house, his mind reeling with seeing her again. Yes, Mallory had grown up in the house, but she hadn't been back in years. It was strange her coming back after all this time, especially since none of her family remained in the area. After her brother had murdered three people and she continued to claim his innocence, Mallory broke off their wedding engagement and never looked back. He hadn't meant to hurt her feelings by not standing up for her brother, but he believed it would be crueler to give her false hope. Sam had committed robbery in the past. Three dead bodies, the murder weapon and one of the victim's jewelry were found in his car. Sam probably hadn't meant to kill anyone but had panicked when he was caught stealing. If he was innocent, why did he run? Sawyer had always spoken his mind and tried to be gentle, but he hadn't expected Mallory to break up with him and leave the area. He believed in working problems out, but it was obvious she hadn't believed their relationship was worth it. Even with tumultuous waters under the bridge, it didn't give anyone the right to harm her. "Did someone take a shot at you?"

In the light from the flames, he could see her frown. "Yeah. After he blew up my Jeep. He was under the tree out there." She pointed to the large pine.

"Have you called for help?"

"Yes. But you should know it will take a little bit for them to get here, especially in this weather."

"There a power line down on the highway, so it may take even longer. I can check things out if you want me to." He knew before he made the offer she would turn him down. Mallory had been in law enforcement when they had dated, and she didn't like to accept help.

"Uh, yeah. Like I said, he's already shot through the

living room window. I don't know if the guy walked here or has some kind of transportation. Do you have a weapon with you?"

"Sure." Sawyer almost always carried, but he was surprised Mallory agreed to have him look around the place. "Are you coming with me?"

"I'll stay in the house. If you see the man, don't feel like you have to approach him. I just want to know if he's still here. And Sawyer…be careful."

"I'll be right back." He unholstered his .45, opened the door and waited a couple of seconds before stepping outside. Mallory surprised him. What was wrong with her? Before she would've been the first one out the door. If there was a shooter outside, she probably would have already arrested him.

He couldn't think about that right now. As he came to the corner of house, he noticed tracks in the mud. Large—the size of a man's shoe—and looked like the sole of a hiking boot. One set went around the house and the other went in the direction of the pine tree Mallory had indicated. He could be wrong, but the tracks looked like the same shoe, meaning there was only one person hanging around the house.

He slid along the siding and moved under a mimosa tree. The branches were bare, but it still provided cover. Mainly, he wanted to get away from the burning Jeep so he wouldn't be easily seen. For five seconds, he surveyed his surroundings. He didn't detect movement, nor were there any tracks under the mimosa or nearby yard. There were two more trees, although smaller, that stood between him and the towering pine. If he could get to that tree, he believed he could tell which way the guy went.

Quickly, he moved to the first tree and stopped. He

looked around without seeing anything and then stepped to the second tree. Raindrops fell from the limbs above, pelting his cowboy hat. The pine was ten yards aways, but something shiny glistened on the ground. It was probably a shell casing.

This time, he moved slowly to the tree, watching for any movement. Yep. It was a shell casing. He bent down and scooped it off the ground when a loud crash had him dropping to one knee to a shooting position.

The sound wasn't a gunshot, but something inside the house.

A child screamed.

Sawyer ran to the back of the house. The back door swung from its hinges, and as he took the steps two at a time, a man in a hoodie carrying a child was running out and plowed into him, knocking Sawyer onto the ground and onto his back.

The child screamed again. Sawyer rolled to his side and grabbed the man's hiking boot. When the guy didn't immediately go down, Sawyer put his weight behind the move to tackle him.

The man dropped the child and almost fell, his hand landing in the mud beside Sawyer. Then he yanked his boot free.

Sawyer got to his feet as Mallory suddenly filled the doorframe and fired twice into the dark where the man had disappeared.

A small trickle of blood flowed from her temple to her cheek and then dripped onto a Texas Ranger badge. A tow-headed boy had his arms wrapped around her thigh in obvious terror.

"What is going on, Mallory?" he ground out as sirens wailed in the distance.

A mixture of fear and anger danced in her brown eyes. "All I know is that I came back to Cedar Hollow tonight, and someone blew up my vehicle, tried to fill me full of lead and attempted to abduct my son on my first night in town. Looks like someone doesn't want me to investigate the three murders everyone believes Sam committed."

"If you just arrived, how would anyone know you were back?"

"I don't know. I stopped by Country Corner to get fuel. I didn't go inside because Maverick was asleep and it was raining, but I noticed there were several people sitting at a booth. Maybe someone recognized me."

He wasn't sure the attack happened because of the murders, but he knew better than to argue. The truth was, he didn't need to alienate her now that she'd returned to investigate. His gaze went back to the boy attached to her limb. Mallory had a son. A sudden coldness hit him at his core. That shouldn't surprise him, but it did. Five years ago, he'd thought it would be him and her getting married and starting a family.

As the reflection of the red and blue swirling lights filtered through the trees, the adrenaline rush of the danger was replaced with dread. Just because her brother had caused pain in Cedar Hollow didn't mean he wouldn't do his part to protect Mallory and her son.

"I intend to find out who attacked me, and then I will learn who really killed those three people." Her gaze penetrated his. "It's time this case be fully exposed, and it seems like someone doesn't want me to live that long."

TWO

The fire truck pulled down the drive first, followed by the paramedics. She noticed Sawyer had stepped back, giving them room. She was glad he'd backed off for he made it difficult to think clearly. As always, he was dressed in jeans, boots and his cowboy hat. She'd always been attracted to his rugged looks.

The first minutes after arriving in Cedar Hollow had left her head spinning. First the attack, and then Sawyer showed up. Neither had been expected. There was no need for Mallory to direct the fire department to her burning Jeep, but the paramedics made their way over to her.

"Is anyone hurt?"

"We're both fine." Mallory didn't recognize the young first responder. That was not surprising considering she hadn't stayed in touch with hardly anyone from Cedar Hollow, except for Mrs. Lansbury and a couple of people she followed on social media. One person she followed was State Trooper Jared Ballenger who she'd partnered with her rookie year. The other was LeAnn Wiggins, who she had been friends with throughout high school.

"How are you doing, sport? My name's Tim," the paramedic addressed Maverick.

Her son moved farther behind her. Mallory said, "He's

frightened because someone tried to abduct him." She glanced at Maverick. "Tim is here to help. I'm not going to let anyone take you." She patted him on the back, trying to reassure him. "You can talk with him."

"Were you hurt?" Tim asked.

"My arm." Maverick held up his left arm.

Mallory's chest felt heavy like a Brahman bull was sitting on it. She hadn't even realized he'd been hurt.

The paramedic felt the limb and turned it over. "I don't think it's broken, but we can transport him to the hospital to be certain."

She didn't believe it was seriously injured, but she wouldn't forgive herself if she were wrong. If her Jeep wasn't burned to a crisp, she would drive Maverick herself instead of putting him in the ambulance. She would do anything to lessen his fear. "Okay. Since my Jeep is not taking me anywhere, I guess we'll go with you."

"Yes, ma'am." Tim nodded.

Sawyer moved up beside her. "I can take you to the hospital if you want."

"That's not necessary," she answered instantly.

He put his hands in the air. "You know best. Just thought it might not be as scary for your boy."

Smoke rose into the damp night air, but the flames were gone. This far out in the country there were no hydrants, but the fire trucks had a large portable tank of water.

She knelt beside Maverick and didn't mind that her knee sank into mud. "How bad does that arm hurt, Mav?"

"Not much." He shrugged and then pointed at Sawyer, who had walked over to greet a deputy who'd just arrived. "Who's that man?"

Her breath hitched. That was a bigger question than she

planned to answer right now. "His name is Sawyer. Did he scare you?"

"No." He shook his head. "He knocked the bad man to the ground."

"You're right. I'm glad he did."

"Me, too." Maverick nodded big.

Sawyer talked with the deputy and then looked her way.

"I changed my mind, if that's okay. We'll hitch a ride with you, Sawyer."

"Good. You two can wait in my truck. It should be warm."

"Thanks." They climbed into the blue 4x4 Ford truck with the heat blowing high. She shook out her shirt so hopefully it would dry quicker. The leather seats must've been heated because she warmed instantly. Mallory would've liked to believe if Sawyer hadn't been there that she still would've been able to catch the man and stop him from kidnapping Mav, but she wasn't certain that would have happened. Sawyer was the only thing standing in the way of the abductor getting away with her son.

Their son.

Sawyer hadn't even acknowledged he had a son, but she didn't want to ask him why in front of Maverick. She had been raising Mav on her own without the help of Sawyer or any family. It had been tough at times on her, but harder on Maverick. Not that a four-year-old understood what he was missing out on, but Mallory did, and it broke her heart. One day, he'd want to know why Sawyer had chosen not to be a part of his life.

Mallory couldn't fathom what someone was doing on the farm, and if Maverick wasn't with her, she would've stuck around to make certain no one was on the property. But she couldn't take that risk.

"Are we staying at the farm tonight?" Maverick asked.

"No, honey, I'm afraid not. We should be able to return in the morning as long as we have electricity."

He cocked his head at her. "Why?"

Lately, that had been his favorite question. "Because the lights wouldn't work. Or the heat. We wouldn't be able to see to get around."

"You have a flashlight. And I have my coat."

She smiled and shook her head. "I'm sure that sounds like fun but not to Mom. We get to stay in a hotel, though. We can return to the farm tomorrow."

"Will the bad man be here again?"

"No. I'll make sure of it." She just hoped she could keep her word.

Once the fire was completely out and she had answered the questions of the deputy, it was past eleven o'clock. She was running on fumes.

Sawyer hurried over to his truck and climbed into the driver's side. "The deputy will holler at you in the morning if he has any more questions."

"Okay."

He glanced at her as he pulled down the driveway. "I don't mind helping you figure out who is behind this. You know our family started Cantrell Security and Investigations. All of us would help you, not just me."

"I appreciate it, Sawyer. But I'm here to look into the deaths of the brother and sister, Tilda and Phillip Pennington, and William Newport. Official Texas Ranger business."

His face tightened for just a second. "I still don't mind. So, to the hospital?"

She looked over her shoulder at Maverick in the back seat. "How is your arm feeling?"

"It's okay."

"It doesn't hurt?"

He poked his arm and moved it like Tim the paramedic had. "Nah."

"That's great." She glanced back at Sawyer. "I'm probably being overprotective, but I'd rather be certain."

"No such thing as being overprotective of your kid. This time of night, it shouldn't take long." Even though his words were sympathetic, his jaw tightened a tad.

What was that about? She would ask him, but Maverick was going through a stage of listening to everything a person said and asking questions. She hoped it was a stage. Now to get her mind back on the attack. "Deputy Jenkins asked me if I recognized the attacker. I didn't. Did you?"

He shook his head. "It was hard to tell with the hood covering his face. He was wearing jeans and muddy hiking boots and was solidly built."

"I noticed that, too." She tried to recall what she'd seen of him, but everything had happened so fast. "A second before he hit me, he turned his head, and I glimpsed cropped hair. Also, he moved quietly, and confidently."

"You're thinking he's no amateur."

"It happened fast, but, yeah, that was my impression."

Sawyer frowned. "The man wore a pinkie ring. I saw it when his lost his balance and his hand landed in the mud beside me."

"Was there anything special about it?" She hadn't noticed a ring, but everything had happened so fast. "Like that would lead us to him?"

"I don't think so. I barely saw it, but it was black and gaudy. If there were words on it, I didn't see it."

"At least that's something."

Several minutes later, they pulled up to the ER at Cedar

Hollow's small hospital. Even though it was a rural medical center, she believed the care was good. Sawyer was right, there was no one in the waiting room and the nurse took Maverick to a room immediately.

Dr. Bourg, who Mallory remembered from when she needed stitches after a skateboard accident when she was twelve, was on call. After a quick physical exam, and Maverick saying nothing hurt, the doctor told them he didn't believe anything was injured. She could give him Tylenol for the pain if his arm started to ache.

In less than forty minutes, they were back in Sawyer's truck. She felt kind of silly for bringing Maverick to the ER, but she was glad he was okay. She didn't like to think about what could've happened if Sawyer hadn't been there. "If you can drop mc off at the hotel, that would be helpful."

"Blue Door Inn?"

"Yep. I figure it's a little late for Rosie's Bed and Breakfast."

Sawyer nodded. "I'm glad your boy wasn't injured."

"Me, too." What was up with him saying *your* boy? Again, it was a conversation for later. "I deal with danger every day, but never where Maverick is in danger. I may've overreacted."

"No such thing," he repeated.

"I wished Evie was here." Maverick kicked his feet restlessly in the back seat.

"She has to work tomorrow." Mallory smiled and then looked back to Sawyer. "Evie Clark is Maverick's sitter and Texas Ranger Jim Clark's mother. The woman watches two other kids of people who worked in the Texas Rangers' office. She loves children and is grandmotherly. I couldn't have asked for a better person to care for Maverick while I'm at work. Not only is Evie good with kids, but she understands the hours of the Texas Rangers and knows there will be times when a field agent will be called away on a case and need to extend the normal business hours."

"Sounds like she's the perfect person to watch your son. Can I ask—"

He stopped short, but Mallory could imagine what he was going to ask. "Later. I'd like to talk to you when there's not listening ears."

Sawyer stuck his hand in the air. "I understand."

Did he really? She certainly didn't understand why, when she had texted and written him to tell him about Maverick, he hadn't responded. Didn't even ask for pictures after he was born. Why? She had certainly expected him to take more interest in their child, then and now.

He pulled under the covered drive of the Blue Door Inn. It was an older hotel that hadn't been remodeled in twenty years, but it was clean and located in downtown Cedar Hollow.

She shoved her irritation aside for the moment. "I appreciate the lift."

"Will you need a ride in the morning?"

"God willing, I plan to rent a vehicle first thing in the morning. We should be fine. Thank you again." She hurried to the back seat and unbuckled Maverick. "Come on."

They hurried to the building, and she could feel Sawyer watching them as she dashed inside the hotel.

The man behind the counter said, "Mallory Foster. Is that you?"

"Yes, sir, Mr. Powell. It's been a while." The headlights shining through the miniblinds moved across the panel wall, indicating Sawyer had pulled away. She almost regretted telling him she didn't need help in the morning.

"It sure has. Haven't seen you since your brother murdered those—uh, since he died." Mr. Powell glanced across the counter at Maverick. "Hey, who's this you have with you?"

Mallory was sure the older man meant no harm because it was accepted in Cedar Hollow that Sam was a killer. She had no desire to discuss her brother or her son. "I need a room for one night."

The man's smile vanished. "Fine. Sign here, and here's your key."

The Blue Door Inn was a single story, so at least they didn't have to lug any luggage up the stairs. What was she thinking? They had no luggage. Everything they had brought with them had burned inside the Jeep. Thankfully, she had her debit cards in her jeans pocket. Before she left the lobby, she asked, "Do you have any toiletries, as in toothbrushes, toothpaste and saline solution for my contacts?"

He nodded toward a closet-sized room. "There's a vending machine."

"Thanks." She tossed him a smile even though it felt like he was being reluctant to help. Maverick walked beside her into the small area. Most of the vending machine slots were empty, but at least there was toothpaste. They would just have to use their fingers to get their teeth as clean as possible, and she'd have to store her contact lenses in water. It wasn't ideal, but it'd have to do.

She also purchased a bag of trail mix. A quick check showed the item wasn't expired, and she was relieved because Mav wanted a snack most nights.

When she opened the door to her room, she was pleased it didn't smell musty and the white comforter looked new. The blue-and-green-swirl carpet could've been updated, but all she wanted was a safe place for them to stay tonight. Clean was the icing on the cake.

"Where's my pajamas?" Maverick asked.

She patted him on the back. "Sorry, hon. Our bags burned in our Jeep. We'll buy more clothes tomorrow. For tonight, take off your shirt and sleep in your jeans."

"And my shoes, too?"

"That won't be necessary. Remove them." She smiled. Even though Mav had been shaken up after the man tried to run off with him, it amazed Mallory how quickly kids recovered. She almost envied her son's innocence, for she knew the danger was not over. If whoever attacked her had something to do with the three murders, then the attacks would not stop.

It only took ten minutes for them to get ready for bed. As practiced, Mallory knelt beside her son to say prayers.

He clasped his hands together and began his prayers as always. "Bless Mama and me, Evie and Lollie. Thank you for Jesus." Then he added, "And thank you for the cowboy who knocked down the bad man. Amen."

They both crawled into bed, Mallory thinking about Mav's prayer. He always mentioned Evie and Lollie, Evie's beagle, in his prayers. This was the first time he mentioned anyone else. She would need to tell him about his dad.

"Mama?"

"Hmm?"

"Is the cowboy a Texas Ranger like you?"

She glanced his way and took in his shining brown eyes. "No, honey. He wears a hat and is a cowboy. He used to be a state trooper, though."

He nodded. "He should be a Ranger. He'd be good at it."

"I think you're right. Now get to sleep." Heaviness weighed on her as she tried to get comfortable. When she came back to Cedar Hollow, she half expected some people might not be friendly, like the Penningtons' parents or the Wilson family. But she hadn't expected to be attacked on her first night in town. Was it possible the man who'd tried to take Maverick had nothing to do with Sam's death or the others? She had only been with the Texas Rangers for a year and had only worked cases with other field agents, so she wouldn't think the man at the farm had anything to do with recent cases.

She'd been a Texas State Trooper for eight years and had worked many cases. But for someone to follow her to Cedar Hollow? That seemed too inconvenient if the person wasn't from this area. The person had to be tied back to Sam and the murders.

Her heart told her Sam hadn't killed anyone. And if that was true, whoever had didn't want her investigating the case. That was evident.

Finally, her eyes began to get heavy. She said her prayers and thanked God for keeping them safe. Then she asked that he watch over them. She had more work to do tomorrow, and she needed his protection more than ever.

And she needed to find the courage to talk with Sawyer about their son.

After Sawyer dropped Mallory off at the Blue Door Inn, he drove up and down the streets of Cedar Hollow. Being that it was a rural town, it didn't take long. He didn't know what the man who'd tried to kidnap Mallory's son drove. The guy had hit Sawyer and took off so fast, he didn't get a good look at his face under the hoodie.

Guessing by the impact, the man was of average height and athletic. Probably not over forty, but Sawyer was only surmising.

He still couldn't believe Mallory had a son. She must've married someone right after she left Cedar Hollow. After she'd broken their engagement, he had figured she would come back once she had time to accept her brother's part in the murders and his tragic death. Maybe that's why she didn't return. She met someone. That would make sense, even though the thought made his gut tighten into a ball.

He couldn't fault her for defending her family. If one of his brothers had done the same thing, he would want to defend them. He hoped he wouldn't refuse to listen to reason, though. Mallory was the most stubborn person he knew. Once she got something in her head, she stuck to her guns.

For the third time, he drove by the Blue Door Inn. He had watched Mallory and Maverick go into room twenty-three. All the lights appeared to be off, and he hoped they both got some sleep tonight. The parking lot still contained the same seven vehicles as before. A bookstore and an antique store shared the same building behind the inn but faced another street. He drove around the block once again. No one was parked at the bookstore.

It was past midnight, and he'd gotten little sleep last night. He knew he should go home. Mallory was a Texas Ranger now and could take care of herself. They had worked together as state troopers for three years before she moved to West Texas. It took a minimum of eight years working law enforcement experience and at least a State Trooper II rank to become a Ranger, and he knew Mallory had talked about becoming one when they dated. He was impressed that she had pursued her dream, even though it must've been tough while raising a child. Her accepting his help to check out the premises at the farm returned to his mind. It made sense now that he knew she had a child who was depending on her for his safety.

He pulled into the parking lot at the nutrition drink store next door. It only had a drive-through and wasn't much bigger than a food truck. He could watch the parking lot and see if someone pulled up or approached Mallory's room.

He laid his seat back and settled in. If he wanted to stay awake, he could've gone down to the all-night convenience store for some coffee, but he hated to leave the inn unwatched in case the guy returned.

His family was in the security business. He and four of his five siblings had started the business after his dad, a Texas Ranger, died on the ranch.

He called his brother Hawk to tell him what was going on.

Hawk seemed unusually quiet after Sawyer explained the situation. "What is it? Is something else going on?"

Clive, brother number three, had just gotten married, and he and his wife had a baby girl. Sawyer was happy for him, and he, Hawk and Cash had all agreed to give Clive a couple of months' reprieve from the business while he enjoyed his new family. Currently, Clive's family were on short vacation to South Carolina to visit his wife's brother.

"Be careful, brother. You and Mallory have a rocky history."

Sawyer was exhausted and concerned for Mallory, and he didn't swallow down the irritated retort. "Come on, Hawk. Don't do this. Mallory and my relationship was over years ago. I'm just checking in like I always do. Besides, now she has a kid to look after. What do you want me to do? Turn away?"

"Calm down."

He clenched his jaw. Yeah, like telling him that would work.

"That's what I'm talking about." Hawk chuckled. "Ever

since she broke the wedding engagement, you've never moved on."

"I've dated."

Hawk kept talking like Sawyer hadn't said anything. "I'm not asking you to turn your back on your old love. Like you said, she has a kid. If there are any unresolved feelings for her, you need to get them settled. We have a safety-first motto for a reason. I'm working the Gonzales case, but I'll be glad to switch clients with you if it'd make it easier."

"I'm capable of protecting Mallory while keeping my emotions in check." He tossed the last comment with a slight sarcastic tone. After agreeing to let Hawk know if he needed help, Sawyer disconnected.

Annoyance settled on him as he thought about Hawk's advice. His brother was only trying to help, but Sawyer didn't need to be reminded of his and Mallory's failed relationship. It still ate at him the way she left after breaking off the engagement and didn't so much as try to stay in contact. Their last conversation ended with her telling him she could never marry a man who refused to stand by her side. That he could at least help investigate even if not in an official capacity.

He'd argued that there was nothing to investigate. After discovering the three dead bodies, a search of Sam's Nissan Titan produced the gun that ballistics proved killed Phillip Pennington and Wilson Newport. Tilda Pennington had been hit in the head. Tilda's jewelry had been in Sam's glove box, along with seven hundred dollars in cash. Evidence at Tilda's house proved the three victims were killed there before being moved. Even though all three victims were dead and couldn't give a statement, investigators believed Sam broke into the Pennington house thinking no one was home. Tilda caught him in the act, and he killed her after a struggle. Then Phillip and Wilson came in, leaving Sam with no choice but to shoot them. He threw them into the back seat of his truck and drove them to Dead Man's Curve, where he planned to get rid of the bodies. But his adrenaline must have been running amok after the murders, causing him to drive too fast and lose control.

The evidence was stacked against Sam. To make matters worse, Sam had been caught stealing from a neighbor three years prior, even though charges were never filed. Mallory had wound up paying for the stolen goods plus an extra five hundred dollars so the neighbors would drop the charges. Sam was supposed to pay Mallory back. Sawyer didn't know if her brother kept his end of the bargain, and Sawyer never asked her about it again.

He and Mallory rehashed the case many times. Mallory always clung to: "I know my brother. He's not capable of murder. He had a good job and was planning to ask Kari to marry him. Why throw it all away for less than a thousand bucks?"

Sawyer's go-to reply was, "Three dead bodies were in his truck."

Sawyer wrestled with the *why* question. Sam was on the right track, and he wasn't in debt that they could find. Investigators had looked at his financial records and didn't uncover any outstanding debts. The only thing Sawyer could figure out was he needed a down payment or deposit on a house so he and Kari could get married. Or maybe take a nice honeymoon.

Maybe if Sam had never gotten in trouble for stealing from a neighbor three years prior to the murders Sawyer would've believed in his innocence. Every time he thought about Sam, he asked himself if he could be wrong. Possibly... And then the next follow-up question he asked himself was, if it wasn't that he was in love with Mallory, would he consider Sam's innocence? No.

It was common for family members to doubt their relative's guilt. Maybe he should've been more patient with Mallory, but he still believed she would have to come around to facing the facts. She refused.

As he stared at the dark window of room twenty-three, he realized now might be a good time for her to come to that conclusion and begin the healing process.

Then, hopefully, they could become friends again and tear down the impenetrable wall that Mallory had built.

First, they needed to thwart any more assaults. It was possible that tonight had nothing to do with the murders from five years ago. But if the attack tonight had something to do with Sam and the past, then it stood to reason Mallory and the boy wouldn't be safe until the man was captured.

THREE

Mallory awoke before the sun was up. She padded to the restroom and splashed water on her face and used her fingers to comb her hair. She couldn't wait for the store to open so she could buy a few things to make her feel normal.

When she came back out, she glanced out the window and saw Sawyer's blue truck was still parked at Nina's Nutritious Drinks. Not able to sleep well, she had gotten up three times in the middle of night and had seen his truck. Even though she didn't feel like it was necessary to be watched over, she appreciated he cared enough. Being on her own for the last five years had made her miss being part of a family.

She needed to find a vehicle to rent as soon as possible. The only place in Cedar Hollow to rent from was the local used car dealership. They probably were not open until eight, but maybe the service department would open earlier.

A knock on the door had her drawing her weapon and glancing out behind the curtain. Sawyer.

She opened the door.

"Good morning. Hope you don't mind, but I saw your light on. Would you like to get some breakfast and then I can take you to Roy's Auto?"

Maverick sat in bed and rubbed his eyes. "Is it morning?"

Sawyer smiled. "It is. Are you hungry? I was hoping your mom would agree to let me pick up some doughnuts for all of us."

Her son perked up. "Can we, Mom?"

She tried not to eat junk food because working inconsistent, long hours made it easy to have a diet of quick and unhealthy food. However, she said, "That sounds good to me, too. It's been forever since we had doughnuts."

It only took a couple of minutes to leave the hotel. Sawyer drove through the drive-through and ordered a variety of pastries. Maverick sat in the middle of the back seat eating his chocolate donut with sprinkles and milk. Mallory chose a doughnut that was cream filled. She'd pay for this later during her workout if she found the time.

She licked her finger after the last bite. "I need to pick up a booster seat at the store."

Sawyer glanced her way. "I can take you. The store is open, and we have another thirty minutes before Roy's opens."

"I'd appreciate that. I have a lot to do today." It didn't take long to pick out a few basic clothes, toiletries, a booster seat and a pack of her Trident Tropical Twist flavored gum. She would stock up on food later once she had a rental car. After they left the store, Sawyer took her to get a vehicle. The loss of her Jeep made her feel sick, for she'd driven it for the past two years and was used to it. She'd paid extra to get good off-road tires and had just had the vinyl top replaced. The car lot didn't have similar SUVs, but they did have a base four-door white truck with four-wheel drive. It didn't have the whistles and bells, but she just needed to make it through the next few days until she could purchase another vehicle.

After the service manager handed her the keys, Sawyer put Maverick's new booster seat in the truck, while she put the shopping bags in and popped a stick of gum in her mouth.

He asked, "Are you still chewing that citrusy gum?"

"It's always been my favorite." Ever since she was a teen and had spending money of her own, she always kept a pack available.

"I would've thought you would've changed flavors by now, but you've always been a creature of habit." He shook his head. "Where are you going now?"

Sawyer was right about her being a creature of habit. Knowing what to expect brought her comfort, even to the simplest things. "I'm going back to the farm. I'm calling the electric company right now to make certain everything is turned on. If there's a problem, I want to take care of it while I'm in town."

"You don't mind if I follow you there?"

"Of course not. I need to have a talk with you anyway. That would be a good time."

"That's the second time you've said you want to talk with me. Is something wrong? Or did you learn something new on the murders?"

She shook her head. "We need to talk about the past."

He looked over his shoulder as a silver sedan drove into the car lot and parked in front of the sales department. A lady with gray hair got out and hurried into the office. He turned his attention back to her. "Okay. I don't like so many people coming and going, especially since we don't know what your attacker is driving."

"I agree." As soon as she got into the truck, she called

the electric company. The woman on the phone told her the service was on. She thought about this as she headed toward her parents' old farm place. Either the storm had knocked it out or the man who was there had turned it off at the breaker box. She felt like he was the one who had followed her for several miles, but maybe he was already at the house, waiting.

Still, that made no sense. No one from Cedar Hollow should've known she was coming. The only place she'd stopped was the large all-night gas station. She had picked up sandwiches and apple slices to go for her and Maverick through a drive-through. And they split a delicious snickerdoodle cookie. There had only been a couple of people in the place that late. It was possible someone had seen her at the diner and followed her.

"Is the cowboy coming, too?" Maverick looked over behind them.

"Turn around, honey." She waited for him to listen. "Yes, he's coming over."

"Good," he said happily. "I like him."

Mallory didn't respond, but guilt that Maverick didn't know his daddy weighed on her. It hadn't been fair to their son for Sawyer not to be a part of his life. But Sawyer made his decision when he chose to ignore her repeated attempts to tell him about the pregnancy, and then about Maverick's birth. His lack of response had cut deep. This was on the heels of losing Sam and her mom. Her dad moved away and married a woman who had three kids still at home. It was like her dad was glad to put his past behind him, including her, and start over. Sawyer wanted her to put Sam's case behind her and everyone in Cedar Hollow made it clear they believed Sam had received his justice by being killed. Or maybe they just held it against her that she believed there was a cover-up and her brother had been the scapegoat.

Either way, Mallory had struggled with the way everyone had treated her, but especially Sawyer. She'd hid away in her own world after her brother's death. If Sawyer would've just told her he would help her learn the truth, then things might have been different. But he hadn't. Knots still formed in her stomach at the hurt that had caused.

After she had Maverick and settled into the community, her life slowly got back on track. Evie was a great sitter and treated her like family. Mallory worked toward joining the Texas Rangers, something Deacon Cantrell—Sawyer's dad—had persuaded her to seek. With only 166 field agents in the entire state, she'd always viewed the Rangers as the most sought-after position in law enforcement. There was a minimum requirement of eight years with the Texas Department of Public Safety to qualify. Finally, a year ago, the Texas Rangers hired her. She became a Christian and started going to worship services.

When she was finally able to request the case file, she found a few inconsistencies. A follow-up phone conversation with one of the witnesses, the victim's neighbor, let her know there had been a dark two-door sports car parked at the Pennington house that night that didn't belong to any of the victims or Sam. Someone being at the scene of the crime meant possible other suspects. The second thing was the anonymous email that claimed the murder weapon was missing from the evidence room. It might be sloppy work at the police department evidence room, or someone might have a reason to want the weapon back. It was enough to convince her lieutenant to agree to give her permission to work on the Pennington and Newport murders, even though he realized her brother had been the prime suspect.

Everything was falling into place.

Now she would clear her family name. If Sam wasn't guilty, that is. If he was, then she would have to accept the truth. She also needed to learn why Sawyer had chosen not to be a part of his son's life. As much as she desperately wanted to prove her brother's innocence, it was more important her son be provided with the best childhood possible.

When she turned on the dirt road that led to the farm, she noticed it was still muddy. The ditches had turned into temporary creeks, and streams of water ran through the pastures. It rarely flooded in the area, and if it did, it was only in a few low-lying places. Thankfully, the truck she'd rented was four-wheel-drive. The road was marked up with tire tracks, but that was probably from last night.

The sun was up, reflecting from the puddles. By the time she pulled into the drive, she'd almost changed her mind about confronting Sawyer about his choice of not being a part of Maverick's life. If he chose not to be a dad, it was his choice.

No. She couldn't put it off. Not anymore. He needed to explain.

As soon as Sawyer got out of his truck, he walked through the house with her and checked the two sheds in the yard. The barn was set about fifty yards back in tall grass. There were no tracks leading to it.

"Doesn't look like anyone is here now," he said. "I'm going to check out the barn."

"Can I play with my new calf?" Maverick asked.

"Sure," Mallory answered. She was glad they'd picked up the plastic cow at the store this morning. "Stay close to me, though."

"Okay." He dropped to the ground and began running his toy across the muddy ground.

Mallory would've reminded him not to get dirty, but there was no use. She walked over to the wooden fence while she kept an eye on Maverick and waited for Sawyer to return. She would've liked to have followed him and talk to him in private, but there was no way she could leave her son out of sight even for a minute. Normally, the country was a safe place to be for kids as long as they didn't get hurt on equipment or fall out of a tree or something.

A couple of minutes later, Sawyer strode back across the pasture toward her. Her chest constricted at the thought of words she would say, but nothing came to mind.

"Did Mrs. Lansbury have access to your barn while she lived here?"

"I suppose so." She cleared her throat. "Sawyer, I've been meaning to talk with you—"

"Someone's been in your barn recently."

"I need to..." His comment derailed her thoughts. "Wait. What?"

"There's tire tracks, probably from some kind of ATV, and several shoe prints."

She had a hard time focusing. "It was probably from our guy last night."

Sawyer shook his head. "I may be wrong but some look more recent than others. Like some are shallow and others deep in the mud. The weird thing is there are irregular marks that I can't tell what they're from. Is there any reason someone would be using your barn?"

"We have the small lake. Maybe someone has been fishing and storing a small fishing boat in the barn. Mrs. Lansbury may've given permission for someone to store things inside. It's not like it was forbidden in the agreement."

Mallory glanced up and saw her son still playing with his toy.

"Come on." Sawyer nodded toward the barn. "Let me show you, and we'll see what you think."

"Hold on. I can't leave Maverick alone." She lowered her voice so her son wouldn't overhear. "Listen. I need to talk to you about Maverick." Now that she'd made up her mind, she didn't want to delay it another second.

Sawyer sighed. "If you're going to explain about his daddy, I don't need to know. I'm happy you found someone."

"What?" She shook her head. "I didn't find anyone else. Maverick is yours. I need to know why you've refused to be a part of his life."

"What?" His voice came out strained.

She was startled by his loud response. "I sent you multiple texts. You never responded."

His eyes grew large. "No, you did not. If you're pulling my leg, it's not funny."

"Mom."

She turned around. "What is it, Mav?"

"That man." He pointed toward the trees to the right of them, about forty yards away.

She and Sawyer exchanged looks.

Mallory hurried toward her son, who was on his knees in front of a large mound with his toy calf.

Sawyer was right behind her.

Several gunshots rang out from what sounded like an automatic rifle.

"Get down." She tackled Maverick behind the mound and slid her gun from her waistband. Sawyer hit the ground beside her. The shot seemed to come from the east line of trees. "Do you see him?"

"No." He looked over the mound, and a shot kicked up dirt between them.

Maverick huddled in a ball at her knee, and her heart went out to him. She glanced at Sawyer. "We need to take cover."

"I'm calling for backup." He quickly texted someone. "Besides the mound, there is no shelter unless we make it to the barn. The house is too far away. I can cover you while you make for the barn."

"I can't risk Maverick getting hurt."

"I agree. That guy's gun is more powerful than ours, and he has the protection of the trees."

A hooded man with a rifle sprinted closer, behind a tall oak tree. He looked to be the same sturdy built guy from last night.

She fired a shot, but her target was already in position. She looked over her shoulder. Her daddy's old Ford tractor with the cab sat behind them. The back tire was low.

Sawyer saw what she was looking at. "Go. If you stay low, you'll be protected most of the way."

"Stay with me, Mav." She pointed. "We're going to get in that tractor."

"Okay."

She grabbed his hand and kept him on her left side, away from the gunman. Sawyer opened fire.

Numerous shots blasted through the country's silence, but she kept her eye on the rusty tractor. Maverick's foot slipped in the mud, but she pulled him along and didn't allow him to fall. As she neared the farming equipment, a ding hit the metal. The bullet was way too close. They hit the ground on the far side, behind the tractor tire.

She glanced back. Sawyer was penned down. Shots continued to ring out. Some from the oak tree and others behind the barn.

Two shooters? One of them must've been hiding in the barn when Sawyer checked it out.

If the two men continued shooting, Sawyer would be out of ammunition soon if he wasn't already. She had to do something.

She glanced up at the tractor. It hadn't been used in a while, but they'd used it to bale hay or feed the cows in winter. Maybe it still ran.

Sawyer glanced at her, and she motioned him over.

"Come on, Mav. We're going to go for a ride." Except for the large windows, the cab would provide protection. "I need you to sit at my feet and keep your head down."

They climbed into the cab. Using the seat for cover, she pushed her gun through the cracked window and shot at the man behind the barn. Maverick clapped his hands over his ears and yelled, "Too loud."

She'd hoped to bring her son to Cedar Hollow to meet his dad and clear her brother's name, but in all those plans, she'd not considered Maverick would be in the line of fire.

Sawyer was low on ammunition and was glad when Mallory fired her gun. He sprinted toward the tractor while staying low. Everything in his mind was reeling. He tried not to be distracted, but how could he not be sidetracked? He had a son! She fired several more times, but so did the men. Bullets kicked up mud at his feet. A whizzing sound went past his ear. He dove behind the tractor and then came up on his feet. He climbed on the step and opened the door. He glanced at Maverick, his son, and his stomach twisted. Mallory should've told him. But more importantly, Sawyer needed to keep him safe long enough to get to know him. "Does this thing run?"

"I'm about to find out."

"If we can get to the house, we'll have protection until my brothers get here." The key was in the ignition. He didn't know if the thing still ran or had diesel. Mallory turned the key. The tractor barely turned over. Once. Twice.

"The battery is almost dead," he said. "Keep trying."

"I am." She shoved the fuel throttle to high and tried again. This time it fired up and died.

The hooded man in the trees ran toward the barn. "They're closing in. How much ammunition do you have?"

"I'm out in my service weapon but should have about four shots left in my backup. Come on. Please." She gritted her teeth and turned the ignition again. Black smoke billowed from the exhaust as it puttered to life. She put it into gear, and the tractor revved but didn't move. She put it into Reverse, and it moved a couple of feet. She slammed it back into Forward, and it jumped over the hump and took off across the yard with mud kicking up behind them.

"I only have a couple of bullets left in my gun," Sawyer said. "I have more in my truck."

The little boy sat on his knees at his mama's feet. He must've been scared because he hadn't said a word. For his sake, Sawyer added, "Everything is going to be okay."

"Oh no." Mallory glanced over her shoulder.

Sawyer looked up in time to see both men running across the open place for the house. The other man wore a dark baseball cap. Still standing on the step outside the cab and hanging on to the handrail, he aimed and fired twice.

The man with the cap grabbed his shoulder but continued to run for the house.

Sawyer pulled the trigger again, but the soft click told

him he was out of bullets. "I'm out of ammo. Let me have your gun."

"No way. Switch places with me."

He was capable, but being she was a Texas Ranger meant she shouldn't loan out her service weapon, even if he believed this was extenuating circumstances.

Just as he was about to climb inside, the tractor bounced roughly. The land dropped off at an angle. The back tire dug in, and the front of the tractor whipped sharply to the left, making the chunky piece of machinery lean and the right tires lift off the ground. "Watch out. It's going to roll."

"Whoa!" She tugged the wheel to the right, trying to keep it from rolling down the hill.

Maverick squealed and stood up. Evidently, he tried to get his balance and grabbed the steering wheel.

Mallory said, "Let go, Mav."

The boy looked petrified and didn't release his grip.

The tractor picked up speed down the incline. It hit a slight ditch and then it tilted toward Sawyer again, the other side coming off the ground.

He grabbed his son with his free hand and wrapped an arm around his waist. Sawyer hit the ground with a roll, barely making it out of the way as the tractor turned over and crashed into the mud upside down. Mallory!

Maverick screamed.

Sawyer's chest constricted, making it difficult to breathe. He kept Maverick in his grasp as he began to search for Mallory under the wreckage.

Hawk's black Ford Raptor tore down the long drive, but Sawyer kept clawing at the dirt to get to her. When he saw movement under the twisted metal, he grabbed her hand. "Help is coming. Hang on, Mallory."

"Mama." Maverick's dark eyes stared at Sawyer like he needed confirmation she was alright.

He held Mallory's fingers in one hand and had his other arm wrapped around his son, holding him snug. "Your mama is going to fine, Maverick." His words came out hoarse. "I'm going to keep you both safe."

He just prayed he could keep his promise, or he would die trying.

FOUR

Mallory tried to lift her head out of the deep muck, but something was pinning down the back of her neck. Panic seized her as she tried to inhale air but struggled. She could hear Sawyer saying something but couldn't make out the words.

Mud caked her face and blocked most of her airways. When she tried to take a breath, she again inhaled mud. Using her hand, she swiped at her face, trying to dig out of the mud. She was finally able to get the debris out of the way of her lips, making her cough. But still there was no room for her body to move because of the weight that was on her. She wasn't even certain what was trapping her except it was the tractor.

Where was Maverick? Sawyer had grabbed him before the tractor had rolled. *Please, Lord, let my little boy be safe.* Surely, she would know it if he'd been hit by the tractor.

"I'm going to get you out of there." Sawyer's voice came to her like a beacon. "Be still."

"Where's Maverick?" Her words caught in her throat. She coughed and tried again. Still her voice refused to work. Her heart picked up the pace. She tried to tell herself to remain calm, but she needed to know if her son was okay. Trying to maneuver to give herself more room, she shoved her right foot, but it dug it into the ground. The action did nothing to move her. A claustrophobic type of panic set in. She needed to get out from underneath this piece of machinery. She tried again with her left foot, but it was more pinned down than the other. "Help me."

Her voice came out so garbled she wasn't certain if he could even understand her.

Warmth touched her hand. Sawyer was trying to dig her out. He said, "Don't move."

He had already said that once, but it wasn't in her to remain still. Not when she couldn't catch a breath, and everything in her psyche told her to fight to get out from underneath this hunk of metal.

Another man's voice said, "On three. One. Two. Three."

Ever so slightly, the weight was lifted from her back even though it still pinned her down.

"Again. One. Two. Three." This time when the weight lessened, someone grabbed her hands and pulled until she slid from underneath the tractor. She was free.

Sawyer knelt beside her. "Are you okay?"

"Maverick." She lifted her head and spit what was in her mouth. "Where's Maverick?"

"Emma has him. He is fine."

Emma was Sawyer's kid sister. Mallory scanned the area until her gaze landed on Maverick. He was in the arms of a pretty ombré-blond-haired lady with a brown and black young pup between them. Tears of relief blurred her vision. He hadn't been injured! Her hand shook as she tried to tame her emotions.

Sawyer rested his hand on her bicep. "Are you hurt?"

She gagged as she tried to clear her throat again. "I… I don't think so. I'm not sure." Slowly, she rolled over. Using her hand for leverage, she pushed to a sitting position. She glanced back at the tractor. It had rolled on its side and rested on the cab. If it didn't have a cab attached, she probably would've been killed. She drew a deep breath. "I think I'm fine."

His dark eyes scrutinized her as if he was trying to tell if she was being honest. He squinted as he brushed dirt from her cheek.

So much had happened, her mind was slow to process everything, which was foreign to her. "Where are the shooters? Are we still in danger?"

"They took off when Hawk tore into the drive. They got away." Sawyer's eyebrows knitted in concern. "Are you having a difficult time breathing?"

She swiped at her face again, trying to clean the dirt off. She was surprised how much was caked on. "Good grief. I was struggling to get air, but I feel better now."

"Mom."

Mallory looked at Maverick, and her stomach tightened. Again, the tears pooled in her eyes. She held out her hands. "Mom is okay. Come here."

Maverick hurried over, his gaze not wavering from her face. "You got dirty."

"Yes, I did." A laugh bubbled out, before the seriousness of the moment slammed into her. "You weren't hurt?"

"No." He shook his head and pointed. "The cowboy grabbed me."

"I'm glad he did." If Sawyer hadn't pulled him off, Mav might have been seriously hurt. She looked back to Sawyer as she tried to get on her feet.

"Careful." He grabbed her arm and helped her up, making certain she was stable before he let her go.

Emma and the pup came over. Sawyer's younger sister had grown even prettier over the years. Mallory had heard

Emma had spent four years in the military, so she must be twenty-two or twenty-three now. Her jeans and hiking boots gave her a down-to-earth sort of look. "Are you okay, Mallory?"

"Yeah." She nodded. Even though she was still slightly shaking, she tried not to show it in front of Maverick. "It's good to see you again. You and your brothers have excellent timing. Thank you."

Maverick tugged on Mallory's shirt. "Did you see the dog?"

"I did." She smiled. She bent over and gave the adorable animal a pat on the head. "Is he a German shepherd?"

Hawk and Cash walked up. Hawk said, "Don't get her started talking about Parker. She'll never stop."

Emma slugged him in the belly. "That's not true. I'm going to train him for Search and Rescue."

"Oh, that's great." Emma had spent time in the army training K-9s. Mallory scrubbed the dog on the head. "You're in good hands."

Sawyer cleared his throat. "This is a nice little reunion, but we need to figure out who is trying to take you down and why."

Although she knew he was right, she sent a glare. "You're not listening. I told you someone doesn't want me looking into the murders Sam was blamed for. It's not that difficult to understand."

"Okay. You're probably right." Sawyer put his hands in the air and batted them down. "But we need to make sure."

Cash smiled at her awkwardly. Whether it was because she had bickered with Sawyer, or because he thought she was wrong, she couldn't tell.

She needed to clear the air. "I'm on official business in Cedar Hollow. As much as I appreciate you being here for me and Maverick, I won't allow you to interfere. No amount of denying the facts will convince me to back away, Sawyer."

"I wouldn't think of interfering or trying to get you to back away from this case." His tone held more than a little annoyance. As he turned to walk away, his gaze landed on Maverick. "You're still as stubborn as always, but we need to work together. For everyone's sake."

"I agree. We're going to wait in the truck until the deputies get here." Inwardly, she growled before holding her hand out to Maverick. She'd caught the inference to their son. She'd been taking care of him since before he was born—something that hadn't always been easy. "Come on, Mav."

"Can Parker come, too?" Big brown eyes stared up at her.

It tore at her mama's heart to say no, especially after he'd been in danger. But she couldn't have him relying on the Cantrells yet. They were a close-knit family, and a four-year-old could easily be pulled into their circle. She would've loved him to be a member of the family, but she still didn't know where Sawyer stood. What if he and Mallory couldn't work out a good arrangement for visitation? "Maybe later. He's Emma's dog."

Quiet enough Maverick couldn't hear, Emma stepped along beside her and said, "I don't mind him playing with the dog. It will be good for Parker's training."

"I appreciate it, Emma. It's very kind of you." Mallory stopped beside her rented truck and opened the back door for Mav to climb in.

Emma smiled. "I get it. You have a lot to do, and your homecoming was not exactly welcoming. I've missed you. It's good to see you again."

"Thanks." Mallory drew a deep breath as she climbed

into the truck and started the engine. She'd forgotten how much the whole Cantrell family had meant to her. Emma was a few years younger than her, but they had always gotten along well.

A call to her lieutenant was needed to explain what had happened. Already she felt in over her head. Would he send another Ranger in to help her with the case? Or could she rely on the Cantrell Security team to assist her? After all, Maverick was a Cantrell and would have to get to know his family. When she talked with the lieutenant, she would tell him about the security team.

Sawyer sat at his truck and stared across the yard at her. What was he thinking? She had the feeling she probably didn't want to know. But seeing him again had brought back memories. Some good, some not so good. One thing was certain. The cowboy would do everything in his power to keep her and Maverick safe. Protecting was in the Cantrell blood.

How was she supposed to feel about that? She'd been making it on her own for years now. Did she really want to slip back into working with him? Maverick's boot kicked the back of her seat, and she saw him staring out the window watching his dad. For her son's sake, she'd do anything to keep them safe. Even work with Sawyer.

Sawyer's knee bounced up and down as he tried to calm himself. Mallory had nerve. She'd not only kept her pregnancy from him, but also didn't tell him when she had Maverick. How could she go through that alone and not think he should be a part of it? And then she waltzes back into Cedar Hollow with the boy at her side and tells him he has a four-year-old son.

How could she do that to him? Not only did it make him

angry, but if he was being honest, it hurt his feelings—not that he'd admit that out loud. Had he been such a horrible person she didn't think he deserved to know? He didn't think so.

They'd gotten along before the Cedar Hollow murders—as the killings became known as. Sure, they'd had their arguments, mostly about silly stuff. They were both opinionated and stubborn. That was something he'd always appreciated about Mallory. She could stand on her own two feet. He'd found that endearing most of the time. Right now, not so much.

Deputy Jenkins pulled up beside Mallory's truck, and she got out while not stepping away from the vehicle. Sawyer walked over to help answer questions. He listened while she explained the two men shooting at them, and the tractor rolling over. She told the deputy she didn't see the two men get away.

"I can help with that one," Sawyer said. He pointed to the east side of the property. "According to Hawk, they took off for the trees when he and Cash arrived. They disappeared into the foliage, and then my brothers heard an engine. Hawk checked it out and said it looked like motorcycle tracks. He and Cash are cruising the backroads as we speak."

Jenkins jotted notes on a pad before looking up at Mallory. "This makes the second attack in less than twenty-four hours."

"Yes. I'm aware of that."

He glanced at her Texas Ranger badge. "Are you working with a local agency?"

"Not yet. I'd planned to talk with Chief Trevett at Cedar Hollow Police Department."

Sawyer could feel her hesitation. She wanted to work the

Pennington and Newport murder case, but the attacks on her might require locals to investigate. "Deputy, Cantrell Security is planning on working with the Ranger if she'll have us."

At his glance, Mallory nodded. "Yes. The Cantrells will be working with me."

Sawyer continued, "We will make certain you stay abreast of the situation, like we called this time."

Jenkins bobbed his head. "Okay. I'll let Sheriff Copeland know."

"We appreciate it."

Jenkins surveyed the scene and took more notes and a few photographs. He pointed out several bullet casings, and when he came to the tractor, he looked up at Mallory. "You're blessed to be alive."

She smiled, although Sawyer was not certain she was happy with his comment. "Yes, sir. I am."

Fifteen minutes after the deputy arrived, he got in his vehicle and left.

Sawyer looked at her. "You coming to the ranch?"

"No. I have things to do."

"If you're going to be in danger, let me take Maverick with me." He wanted to let his son meet his mom and see the horses. He wanted his son to be a part of his life.

"No way." She glanced to her truck, where Maverick sat in the back playing something on an iPad. "He's not going to be in danger. I'm going to visit with the chief."

He cocked his head at her and stared.

"Don't look at me like that. I know how to keep him safe."

"So, you normally take him with you when you go to work?"

"You know I don't." She sighed and turned away, breaking eye contact. After several seconds ticked by, she planted her hands on her hips. "I wasn't supposed to be in danger when I came to Cedar Hollow. I was going to investigate. You know, talk to people and go over the case they had against Sam."

"Then it's settled. Either I take him with me to the ranch where I'll keep a close eye on him, or I go with you."

Her shoulders dropped. "You can come with me, but I'm in charge. Got it?"

In charge of the case or their son? He didn't ask. "Got it. I'm not trying to cause you trouble. But I'm not going to sit on the sidelines while someone is trying to kill you and kidnap my boy."

"Okay," she whispered with a glance over her shoulder. "I haven't told him who you are yet. So, keep it down."

"Don't you think it's about time?"

"Yes..." She dragged the word out like it was offensive. "But I didn't believe you wanted to be a part of his life. What age is the best time to tell a little boy that? Two? Three? Four?"

"But I didn't know about him." His heart raced at the comment. "You said you texted me. When was this?"

"About a month after I moved. I kept feeling sick until I finally took a pregnancy test. I texted you three different times."

"I wish you would've contacted my family or something to get ahold of me when you didn't hear back from me."

He removed his Stetson and ran his fingers through his hair. "I never received your texts. There was a time when I dropped my cell phone in the barn, and my horse stepped on it. It cracked my phone. I could still receive calls, but my texts quit coming through. It took me a couple of weeks before I bought a new one."

"How was I supposed to know your phone wasn't working?" Her voice hitched an octave.

"There was no way for me to know you were trying to get ahold of me. I figured anyone who didn't hear back on a text from me would give me a call. You could've called my family."

"That's not fair. I thought you were ignoring me, giving me my answer. I didn't want to involve your family. They can be overwhelming. Not only that, but I sent you a letter."

"To the ranch?" What was she trying to say? That someone in his family had intercepted it?

"No." She shook her head and shrugged. "I sent it to you at the department."

He'd thought she'd always liked his family. There was no way he'd misread that. The drawn look on her face said it hurt her feelings he hadn't responded to her texts. He certainly hadn't done it on purpose. They needed to discuss this more later. "You want to ride with me?"

"Not really. Since I already have Mav's booster seat in my vehicle, we can use it. Besides, I like to drive."

He got in on the passenger side. He wasn't happy, but for now, it was best to let the small stuff slide. They had too many important things to work out. Oncc they were on the road, he turned around to look at his son. He had dark hair, and if Sawyer wasn't mistaken, he also had a small cleft in his chin like he had. The resemblance was so obvious that Sawyer couldn't believe he didn't notice it when he first saw him. "Hey, sport. What are you playing?"

The boy held up the iPad. "The Ranch."

Because of the sun's glare, Sawyer couldn't make out anything but bright colors. "You like farm animals?"

He gave a big nod. "'pecially horses." He held up a baby red and white plastic calf toy. "I want a horse."

Mallory said, "He loves the calf, but the store was out of horses. He would love the whole collection."

"Maybe your mama will come let you ride one of mine." Sawyer cut his eyes to her, and she stared right back.

"A real one?" Maverick sat straight. "Can I, Mom? Can I?"

"Maybe, but not today." She said the words cheerfully to her rearview mirror before glancing back to Sawyer.

He was glad she hadn't said no. They had so many things to discuss.

"Aw." Maverick slouched his shoulders. "I want to see the horses."

"Mom has work to do first." This time she shot Sawyer a dirty look. "I need to discuss this with Sawyer."

Using Maverick to put pressure on her wasn't the way to work things out, and he didn't want to fight her. He leaned closer. "Sorry 'bout that. I'll ask you next time before I mention anything to him. But I really would like him to see the ranch. I loved growing up with animals."

"I realize that." Her jaw twitched.

He felt like he kept saying the wrong thing. Of course, she knew he loved the ranch and must also realize Maverick would love it, too. Most kids did. The truth was if he wanted a good relationship with his son, that meant working with Mallory—even if she had been the one to break off their wedding engagement.

Several minutes later, she pulled in front of the Cedar Hollow Police Department. It was a small metal building that had been built only a couple of years ago. The volunteer fire department shared the building, making it cost effective for the rural community. "I'll stay here with Maverick while you talk with the chief."

She started to open her mouth but then stopped. "I

shouldn't be long. You have my number if you have any questions."

There was an ice cream concession trailer one block up the street. He leaned in so the boy couldn't hear. "You don't mind if I walk him to the Scooper Dooper, do you? He's not allergic to milk products or anything?"

"That's fine, and I'm sure he'd love it." A smile twitched at her lip before she looked in the back seat. "Sawyer is going to take you to get ice cream."

"Yay!" The boy scrambled to unbuckle.

"We'll be waiting on you," Sawyer said to Mallory before he opened the back door for his son. Sawyer took Maverick's hand, the feeling surreal. He glanced back up, but Mallory had already disappeared into the police station. He knew she was struggling with Sawyer taking an active role in their son's life, but he was glad she didn't fight him on the small request. "What's your favorite flavor?"

"Chocolate." He glanced up at him with big brown eyes. "What's yours?"

"I like them all but am particularly partial to rocky road."

"I want rocky road, too!"

Sawyer's chest constricted. The sweet boy kept a grip on Sawyer's hand. It felt like Sawyer had four years to catch up on everything he'd missed. He couldn't look at it that way or he'd never enjoy the present. As they approached the shop, Cheyenne, the nineteen-year-old daughter of the owner, who'd set up the store to pay for the girl's college, smiled big. "Hey, Sawyer. Who's that big guy you have with you?"

"This is my cowboy friend, Maverick. We'd like two double-dip rocky roads."

"Ooh. Maverick. I love that name."

Sawyer glanced up and down the street. A green motorcycle was parked in front of the Greasy Griddle. He didn't recognize the bike, but there were several people in the area who rode them, especially in the spring and fall. Not only locals, but many people traveling through. Still, this one looked to be a performance bike, which was a little unusual in the area.

Using his cell phone, he snapped a photo of the bike, trying to make sure he captured the license number, but a square hedge blocked his view of the plate. An unfamiliar younger man with a slight stoop and long red wavy hair walked out of the diner and climbed onto the bike. His gaze connected with Sawyer's for a split second before he revved the machine and took off. Sawyer clicked another photo. With Maverick with him, he decided against getting closer for a better shot.

As much as he didn't want to, he needed to help Mallory dig into the five-year-old murder cases if he was going to be able to spend time with his son without looking over his shoulder. Cheyenne handed them their cones. As they turned to walk back to the truck, Maverick held up his hand, and Sawyer proudly took it.

Who would've thought less than twenty-four hours ago Sawyer was on his way home with his future perfectly laid out before him. Now he was a dad and on the most important mission of his life.

FIVE

Mallory drummed her fingers on the counter as she waited for the desk clerk to return. She'd been waiting over ten minutes, and she was beginning to wonder if the woman had taken a coffee break.

The middle-aged woman with curly shoulder-length hair stepped back into the room. "The chief said you can come on back and find the files."

The way the woman said it made Mallory wonder if he had said it ruder than that. Something like, "If she wants it, tell her to find it herself." It didn't matter to her, and she even preferred not having anyone looking over her shoulder. The clerk led her to a room no larger than a closet overstuffed with boxes, and even one plastic tub overflowing with Christmas decorations.

"Will you need my help?" The woman shrugged. "I don't have much of anything else to do."

Mallory started to tell her that wouldn't be necessary, but many times people liked to talk and open up about what they knew. The main thing she wanted to know was if the gun that was used to kill Phillip Pennington and Wilson Newport was still in the evidence room. "I'd appreciate that. I didn't catch your name."

A smile lit up her face. "I'm Cheryl. I've only been in

here a handful of times, but the room doesn't seem to be in any particular order. I've offered to organize it, but the chief said it was unnecessary."

"Yeah, I'm guessing there are not many cases in a department this size. Looks like someone started to alphabetize it. *A* through *J* is on the top shelf."

"I see that. What were the names again?"

"Phillip and Tilda Pennington, and Wilson Newport."

"Hmm." The woman sucked the side of her cheek in. "I guess we can start anywhere."

"I agree. The murders happened five years ago, so I figure the files may be together."

"That would make sense," Cheryl said.

Mallory said, "I'll start on the right side of the room, and you can begin on the left so we don't trip over one another."

She started at floor level and opened the first box. There were several manilla envelopes inside along with several documents not labeled. She quickly scanned the papers but didn't see anything with the Pennington or Newport's names. "I don't remember you from when I lived here. Are you new to the area?"

Cheryl sat on a step stool and placed a box on the floor. "Not really. I grew up here but moved to Mustang, near Oklahoma City, when I was twenty-one. Years later, after a short battle with cancer, my husband died, and I moved back here to take care of my mama. She's eighty-two and doesn't want to leave the house that she's lived in for over sixty years. So as of two years ago, here I am back in Cedar Hollow."

The desk clerk looked to be about twenty years older than herself, so that would explain why Mallory didn't remember her. "I can understand your mom wanting to remain in her home. So, you didn't know any of the victims?"

"Not them. But I knew Evelynn Newport, Wilson's mama. We went to high school together. We were both on the basketball team. She was a couple of grades ahead of me, but being Cedar Hollow was small, I was on varsity as a freshman. I probably should've reached out to her after her son was killed, but I didn't for fear she'd think I was fishing for gossip. Instead, I talked to Rochelle, a mutual friend, who told me all about the killings. I've never met a Texas Ranger before. I didn't even know there were any women agents."

"I get that comment sometimes, but women have been Texas Rangers for almost forty years."

Cheryl smiled. "I must commend you on the achievement."

"Sometimes it still doesn't seem real." Mallory pulled another box from the shelf. She was enjoying her visit, but she needed to hurry and get back to Maverick and Sawyer. If she'd known she was going to be attacked as soon as she returned, she would've found other arrangements for Mav. Emma might help watch him, but she didn't know what the woman had going on these days. She might not have time, and Mallory didn't want to take advantage of Sawyer's family.

They were Maverick's family, too.

The thought came unbidden. She wanted him to be close to Sawyer's family, but at the same time she wanted to protect her relationship with him. Was she being selfish? This wasn't about her. She wasn't going to lose him like she did the rest of her family, even if he did get close to the Cantrells. Honestly, even though she had broken the wedding engagement, after struggling with her own childhood, she realized how important a close-knit family could be.

"I found something." Cheryl handed Mallory a thick manilla envelope with the name Matilda "Tilda" Pennington written in a thick permanent marker.

"This looks like it." She glanced at the box at the woman's feet. "May I?"

"Sure." The clerk pushed it across the tile floor.

Mallory quickly rifled through the box. There was a folder with Phillip's name, but not much else. She rummaged through it again a little slower. There was nothing on Wilson Newport. "I can make copies of everything here, but I feel like there's more. Wilson Newport should be here, too. The gun used in the crime should be here, too. I wasn't planning on it taking this long to find the files."

Cheryl stood. "I can go make copies while you continue to look if that helps."

"That would be wonderful." Mallory glanced at her phone. It was eleven thirty-two. She'd been here over twenty-five minutes. She definitely needed to make other arrangements for Maverick or get someone else to look at the case. No one else would do as thorough a job as she would. That, she was certain of.

She set the Pennington box on the chair and pulled more boxes out that were close to where Cheryl had been working. On the fourth try, she found Wilson's file in a box marked Melinda Hall. A quick glance showed Melinda's case was two years prior to Wilson's murder and had no connection Mallory could find. Whoever was in charge of filing evidence had done a sloppy job.

A stack of folders lay atop of the second shelf, and Sam's folder was in the middle of those. A list of stated evidence was inside, including the Smith and Wesson SD 40 that Sam supposedly had used to shoot the two male victims, crime scene photos, and statements made during the witness interviews. She rifled through several more boxes to see if she could find the gun, but it was nowhere to be found.

Cheryl stepped back into the room. "I made copies of everything."

"Thank you. You've been such a help. The Smith and Wesson used in the murders is listed on the list of evidence, but it's not inside. Do you know where else it might be?"

The clerk shrugged. "Sorry. I don't. Could it have been misplaced in someone else's file?"

"I've looked in some of the other containers but didn't find it." Mallory glanced at the pile of boxes. Surely something so important wouldn't be dropped into another person's file.

"I would've thought you would've been done by now."

Mallory turned at the masculine, gruff voice. "Chief, the boxes are in no particular order, so it took me longer than I'd anticipated. I can't find the murder weapon. Do you know where it is being stored?"

His gaze narrowed. "Not offhand. But we don't leave guns laying around."

Cheryl smiled and quietly dismissed herself from the room. Evidently, the clerk did not want to be on his bad side.

Mallory had dealt with contrary law enforcement before and did her best to be stern, but not antagonistic. She ignored his sarcastic remark. "I made a copy of the files. Is there someone who knows where the rest of the evidence is located?"

"This is it. We're not some fancy department, but we're not a bunch of hillbillies, either."

Actually, he was coming off as paranoid more than contrary, but that didn't mean he had something to hide. Maybe. "It's time for me to go, but I'll check back tomorrow to see if you can locate the weapon," she said.

She restacked the boxes where they had been while he stood in the doorway watching. "I'll let Lieutenant McAllister know the files are incomplete. Thank you."

"The gun should've been there." He said it like it meant she'd missed it.

"Yes, sir." Sometimes it diffused the situation to address the law with respect. Not always, but it couldn't hurt. With the copies in her hand, she walked out of the police department. Sawyer was sitting with Maverick on the tailgate of her truck.

Sawyer glanced at her hands. "I see you got what you were looking for."

"Not everything." She glanced at Maverick. A smudge dotted his check. Using a dry thumb, she attempted to rub it off unsuccessfully. "Did you get some ice cream?"

He nodded excitedly. "I got rocky road like the cowboy."

"That sounds wonderful. Mama's ready to go." Once they were back in the truck, she addressed Sawyer. "Thank you. Hope he wasn't too much trouble."

He waved his hand. "Not at all. Please don't thank me for spending time with him. You know I want to. We need to talk about all this soon."

She backed out of the parking space. Frustration settled on her. Of course, Sawyer didn't need to be told thanks, but she was used to being the only one taking care of her son. Besides Evie Clark, his sitter during work hours, there had been no one else to help her. Having someone else watch him for a few minutes was new territory for her. Normally, when she was at home or shopping, sick or just wanting a moment to herself, Mav was at her side. She didn't mind because that's what being a mom was all about. But still…

"What are your plans now? Did you learn anything new?"

"I need to go somewhere where I can go through the files. I've already gone through most of these files that were sent to me online at the Texas Ranger field office. I won't know until I go through them if there is anything more. I'd intended to be staying on the farm, but now that doesn't sound like a good place."

"Come by the ranch. It only makes sense."

"I'm afraid having people in and out will be a distraction. By the way, the murder weapon is missing, which is the reason Lieutenant McAllister let me reopen the case."

He narrowed his gaze. "That's not good, but how did you know it was missing?"

"When I moved to West Texas, I created pages on social media to help learn information about the case." She shrugged. "I hadn't received useful information until last month when someone, anonymous, emailed me that they heard someone had bragged about using the gun that killed Phillip and Wilson."

"You're kidding me. That would've been useful information. Why didn't you mention that before now?"

"Because I wanted to make certain the claim was credible. Since the gun is listed on the evidence list, but isn't with the other things, I'm assuming the tip is true."

"Have you found out who sent the email?"

Being that Sawyer had been a state trooper and was still in security, she expected him to know it was fairly easy to learn an email sender's information. She sighed. "I have. I knew the person wanted to stay unknown, but if I'm going to reopen the case, it's important information."

"Well?" He waited for her answer.

"I'd rather not say until I talk with her. She may have her reasons for not wanting anyone to know." The email address belonged to Janet Jacobson, a sixty-something-year-old resident of Cedar Hollow who had four kids. Mallory was familiar with Janet's children Randy and Becca because they were close to Sam's age in school. Randy and Sam had hung out some. The other two kids were younger, and she didn't know them.

"Okay." The way he chopped off the word made it sound like he wasn't happy. He looked out his passenger window for a few seconds as if in thought. "You think someone broke into the evidence room?"

"Possibly. Or was let in."

He frowned. "You're saying someone in the police department. You know it's a small department and it's not known for running a tight ship, but that would be pretty careless." His eyebrows arched. "Unless you think something more nefarious is going on."

"I'm not ruling anything out. Evidence might be missing because of incompetence. Or someone knew it was in the storage room and broke in, or maybe the true killer wanted the gun back for some reason.

"I don't know the chief that well. When Sam was accused, Chief Trevett was here. Does Trevett work well with your security team?" She'd found the chief unprofessional, but she didn't want to complain since she'd only arrived and didn't know him.

"He's okay. Always seems a tad annoyed if he's asked to help, but he does a good job for the size of his department. I try to put myself in his position. He'd rather everyone use his department, and he gets defensive like his team is being insulted when someone hires our family, or an outside agency comes in."

"That's a common issue."

As they drove up the street past the ice cream stand,

Sawyer said, "There was a bright green motorcycle that looked like a Kawasaki Ninja parked there. It's gone now."

"I assume you don't recognize who it belongs to."

"Nope. When the owner noticed me staring, he took off. I took a couple of quick photos. I already sent them to Cash. The images weren't clear, but I'm hoping he can enhance them enough to be able to read."

"Good. Thanks." As she drove out of town, she tried to wrap her mind around what all she needed to do. She wanted to interview Kari Bryne, Sam's girlfriend at the time of his death, but she also needed to become more familiar with the witness interviews that were conducted at the time of the murders. "I need a quiet but safe place to work. Any ideas?"

"The office in the barn should give you privacy."

"I told you I'd rather not stay at the ranch." She'd be surrounded by his family, and it'd be impossible to concentrate. She had already made plans to stay at the farm and figured Maverick would have fun playing there. But that was out of the question now. "I wouldn't feel any safer at the Blue Door Inn."

He shrugged. "I don't know what you want me to tell you. You have most of my family at your disposal. My mom, sister and Shaylee the housekeeper… Do you remember Shaylee?"

"Barely. She'd just started working when I moved."

Sawyer nodded. "Any of them would help with Maverick. I wished Holly were here. Then—"

"Wait. Who's Holly?"

"Clive's new wife. She just had a baby. You two would get along, but that's beside the point. Little Jeanine is five months old, and Holly stays home with her, but bakes on the side for the Greasy Diner. Her and Clive are on a family honeymoon right now."

Mallory tried to take it all in. She'd always gotten along with Clive but thought he was a private person. She also noticed how withdrawn he'd been when his ex-wife, Giselle, left him. "Good for Clive."

Sawyer nodded. "Yeah. I've never seen him more content, and I wasn't sure he'd ever get over Giselle. Anyway, we have plenty of people to help you on the ranch. There's a place in Oklahoma, a vacation rental, but it's out of the way and would be inconvenient driving back and forth to interview people."

"You're not getting it, Sawyer. I love your family, and they would be good to me. But they are overwhelming. I would never have a moment's peace. I need to concentrate on the case."

She turned into the main highway out of town and headed west. She didn't know where she was going but didn't want to park to talk. Indecision had never been a problem for her. Why did it decide to pop its ugly head now?

"You're not open to options then." He sighed. "Why don't we leave Maverick with the women at the ranch, I'll go with you somewhere outside of Cedar Hollow, either your parents' farm, or we could find a vacation rental. All you need is an office or place to sit down and go through the files."

She didn't correct him when he called it her parents' farm. Mallory was the rightful owner of the farm since her father gave her the deed six months ago. But Sawyer was right. All she needed was a quiet place to go through the files. Why was she afraid of his family? Because she'd grown close to them and cared about them. They had made her feel part of the family more than her own family had. She wasn't a young impressionable girl anymore. She'd paved her own way and had been doing well on her own.

"Still stubborn I see."

She jerked her head to the side. "I'm thinking."

He had the nerve to smile, which caused the cleft in his chin to become more pronounced. Just like Maverick.

"Okay." She threw her hand into the air. "Since it's after noon, let's grab a quick lunch and go to the ranch. I'll get Maverick settled in with Shaylee or Emma. Whoever has the time. I'd rather you not mention your relationship to him until we tell him."

"After the ice cream, I'm not that hungry, but we need to eat." He gave a slow nod. "If you want to slow play telling my family, fine. But I never thought you were the type to put things off."

"This is important, not something to take lightly." She drove through the drive-through at the Burger Barn. After they were handed two burger bag meals plus a child's meal, she pulled to the curb and passed out the food and drinks.

"You want to do the blessing, Mav?"

He nodded. "Thank you for this burger and for Jesus. Amen."

She glanced at Sawyer, and they stared at one another for a second. What was he thinking? His family had always said grace before meals, so surely he wasn't surprised. She pulled onto the highway toward the ranch, her mood sour as she munched on her food. The conversation about telling Maverick that Sawyer was his daddy wouldn't leave her mind. What was even more frustrating was that Sawyer was right. She was dragging her feet, and it served no purpose. Sawyer's family would find out soon enough, and what did it benefit? Nothing except not to distract her from the cold cases. But already her mind was on his family and not clearing her family name.

Twenty minutes later, as they approached the large entrance of the ranch, she looked into her rearview mirror. "Maverick, we're going to Sawyer's ranch. Okay?"

"Really? Can we see the horses?"

"Yes, we can see the horses." She drew a deep breath and prepared herself to be overwhelmed by the whole Cantrell clan. When she returned to Cedar Hollow, she'd planned to talk with Sawyer and get answers of why he hadn't wanted to get to know his son, but now it's like she'd stepped back in time. Her chest tightened in anticipation. She was determined not to be drawn back in.

SIX

Sawyer knew Mallory was struggling to let him be a part of their son's life. Even though it was annoying that she fought it, if there was a better way, he would suggest it just so she would relax. She pulled the truck around the back of the main house and parked next to his mom's car.

He gathered up the bags of trash from the Burger Barn, and he noticed he was the only one to eat all of his meal.

Mollie Beth ran to the driver's side and barked at the unfamiliar vehicle. Emma walked out of the barn with her pup at her feet.

"Is that a dog?" Maverick tossed his seat belt aside and pressed his nose against the back glass.

"It is," Sawyer answered. "Her name is Mollie Beth." He hurried out of his side in time to see the older golden retriever greet Mallory and Maverick with a hyper tail and her tongue dangling to the side. She was just the right height for her face to be directly in front of Maverick's. Afraid she might make him nervous, Sawyer said, "Sit, Mollie."

The retriever obeyed.

Emma's dog trotted over and licked Mollie on the face before doing the same to Maverick.

"Parker, sit." Sawyer's younger sister hurried over. She put her hand in front of him and lifted it to her bicep. The pup wiggled before sitting on his hind legs. She pushed a clicker and then rewarded the German shepherd with a treat. "Good boy."

Maverick looked up in awe.

"Hello, Maverick," his sister said joyfully. "I'm glad you came for a visit."

"You have two dogs." His son patted Mollie Beth and Parker on their heads at the same time.

Sawyer said to Emma, "Mallory needs some quiet time to study some case files. Are you busy right now?" He could see Mallory in the corner of his eye and noted she hadn't moved away from the truck and held a backpack in her hand.

"Not too much. I just finished a short training session with Parker, and I was about to go inside to make him more treats. I found a new healthy recipe I was wanting to try." She turned to Mallory. "Would you like for me to keep an eye on Maverick while you work? I'm sure the dogs would enjoy the company."

"I'd really appreciate that. I won't be long."

Emma waved her hand. "Don't worry about it. Besides baby Jeanine, it has been a long time since we had a kid on the ranch. I look forward to showing him around. He looks like a cowboy in the making."

Maverick nodded. "Yeah."

"Thanks, sis." Sawyer patted her back before turning to Mallory. "Would you like to come in and say hello to my mom? I'm sure she'd like to see you again."

The corner of her mouth lifted. "Sure."

Sawyer held back a laugh and resisted making a comment about her lack of enthusiasm. All of them walked into the kitchen together. He tossed the trash into the receptacle. Shaylee was sitting at table eating a cookie.

"Mallory, you remember Shaylee. She's still keeping the ranch running for us." Being Mallory was only a couple of years older than Shaylee, he'd always figured they would've been close friends if Mallory had never left. He turned to the red-haired cook as she wiped crumbs from her cheek. "Shaylee, this is Mallory. She's working on a cold case."

Shaylee glanced at the badge on her chest. "Glad to meet you." Her attention turned to Maverick. "And who is this?"

Mallory rubbed him on the head. "This is Maverick, my son."

Our son, Sawyer thought. He didn't like this idea of keeping his identity a secret. He'd just learned about him and already he wanted to announce him to the world. "Emma is going to show him around the ranch. If it's okay with his mama, you could offer him a cookie." He glanced to Mallory.

"Can I have one?" Maverick asked.

"You didn't eat all of your lunch." She visibly sighed. "Since you had ice cream earlier, that's all the snacks you can have before supper. Okay?"

"Okay." He grabbed a cookie.

"Anyone else?" Shaylee held the plate.

Emma and Sawyer each took one. He was surprised when Mallory also took one.

"Oh my. That's delicious." Mallory looked at Shaylee. "You're an excellent cook."

The housekeeper smiled. "Thank you. But Holly made these before they left on their vacation. These are the best I've ever had."

"Where's Mom?" Sawyer figured it'd be better to get the reunion over with. His mom hadn't said much except to offer comfort when Mallory left Cedar Hollow, and Sawyer hadn't been appreciative of her encouraging words back then. He'd been frustrated and embarrassed to be dumped after making wedding plans. Having sympathy seemed to make it worse.

Shaylee said, "She's out for a run."

"Again? I should've guessed." As Emma and Shaylee started to visit, Sawyer nodded toward the living room.

Mallory scrubbed Maverick on the head. "You okay, Mav?"

"Yeah!" Before he was through talking, he hurried to Emma's side, obviously excited about going outside.

When it was just them two, he asked, "Would you rather work in my room, the office or the office in the barn? I'll make certain no one bothers you."

She looked thoughtful and shrugged. "Your room. I won't take too long. I can dig in deep tonight, but I'd rather look over the interviews. Hopefully, I can go start reinterviewing people today."

They went upstairs to the second floor to the third bedroom on the right. He opened the door. Shaylee made the beds, but she didn't touch personal stuff. He had an old pair of boots and a vest in the leather chair. "Excuse the mess."

"No problem. Let me know if Maverick needs anything."

"You know I will, Mal. Sorry. Mallory." The shortened name came out without thought, but it sounded too chummy for how tense she'd been. "Do you need my help? Another set of eyes?"

"I've got it."

"Okay. Please don't hesitate to accept my professional assistance." He shut the door behind him. If only she would trust him to help look at the case with her. When they were both Texas State Troopers, they often talked about cases and shared advice on how to handle things. Rarely did they officially work on cases together, but that didn't mean they hadn't helped one another.

She doesn't trust me.

The thought came to him as he walked down the stairs, and it made him sad. They used to be so close and seemed to be perfect for one another. He didn't believe they could ever have what they used to, but he'd like to see them get along and become friends. If that was possible.

His mom came through the kitchen door, red faced and sweaty. He asked, "Did you have a good run?"

"I did. It makes me feel energetic once I'm done. Maybe not so much at first. Was that a boy out there with Emma and Shaylee near the barn?" She dabbed her neck and face with a towel.

"Yeah. Mallory is here. That's her little boy, Maverick." It felt like a lie to not tell his mom Maverick was her grandson, but he kept his promise not to tell his family until they had time to tell Maverick first.

"Mallory Foster?" Her eyebrows shot up. "I'm surprised. What is she doing here? How are you two getting along?"

"We're fine, Mom. She's here working on a cold case. I'm sure you remember she became a Texas Ranger."

She reached for a bottle of water out of the fridge and took a long swig. "I remember, son. I also remember how close you two were and how it about killed you when she broke off the engagement."

"Hey, you want to go with me to see—" Mallory came into the room but stopped when she saw his mom. "Nora."

"I would hug you, but…" His mom pulled the sweat-ridden shirt away from her skin and fanned herself.

Mallory smiled and held her arms out. "I don't mind."

Awkwardness filled Sawyer until the women broke their embrace.

"It's good to see you," his mom said.

"You, too. You look great, like you're getting in shape."

"Thank you. I feel good." His mom gave her a satisfied smile. "I haven't run in years, but I enjoy how it makes me feel. Well, afterward, that is…"

Mallory laughed.

Sawyer cleared his throat. They didn't have to discuss his mom's new hobby. "I'll go with you, Mallory. Who do you want to go see?"

She glanced around, ignoring his question. "Clive is on vacation with his new wife, so I've seen everyone except for Brock. Where has your little brother been hiding?"

The room grew silent with tension. How did he answer in front of everyone? After several awkward moments, he abruptly said, "He's gone. Who do you want to go see today?"

"Kari Byrne and Dr. Bourg if there's time. Kari's original interview couldn't have lasted over five minutes. She agreed to see me. I'm hoping she can give us more information."

His mom said, "I'm going to get cleaned up. Mallory, can we expect you for supper?"

"Uh, I'm not certain, but I appreciate the offer."

"Thanks, Mom. We'll let you know." He and his mom exchanged glances. He could sense she was concerned for him. As Sawyer followed Mallory out the back door, he felt like everything was put into motion and there was no slowing it down. Maverick was here with his family, but they didn't know he was Sawyer's son. Someone had tried to kidnap his boy and kill Mallory. She was offering to take him with her to investigate a lead. So much was happening, but he'd been in tough situations before.

He needed to talk with his brothers. If someone was targeting Maverick, they needed to know to be on the lookout for anything suspicious and keep an eye on his son. Too much was at stake to let their guard down.

His gaze went to Mallory as she walked toward the barn. The stakes were high for all involved.

SEVEN

Mallory was glad to get out of the house. She loved the Cantrells, but it brought back too many memories. She had planned to be a part of this family when she married Sawyer. What was bad was she'd already felt like she belonged to the family. And then when she broke off the engagement, it also separated her from all of them. She loved his parents and the siblings. It was Deacon Cantrell, Sawyer's dad, who had encouraged her to be a Texas Ranger. It was normal when a relationship didn't work out that it severed ties with more than just than the romantic interest, but it still bothered her.

When she walked outside, she heard voices in the barn and found Maverick standing with the two dogs. "Hey, Mav. I'm going to town with Sawyer. Will you be okay here with Emma and Shaylee?"

"Yeah! Emma is going to let me pet the horses. She said I have to let her help me. Can I, mom? Can I pet the horses?"

"Of course, but you need to listen to Emma and be careful."

"I will."

Sawyer walked up beside her. "I'm sure you remember the dapple is Binion, Clive's horse. And that one over there—" he pointed to the blue-roan "—is mine. His name is Blue Steel, but I call him Steel."

"Wow, he is absolutely gorgeous." Mallory's breath stalled. "I love his black mane and tail with his gray-speckled body. He's the most magnificent horse I've ever seen. Binion is also a pretty guy."

Sawyer's chest puffed slightly. "I've worked hard to build a good herd of horses. Steel is a good-looking fellow."

"Can I ride him?"

"No." Both she and Sawyer answered Maverick in unison. Sawyer went on to say, "Maybe some other time when your mom or I am with you."

Maverick dropped his head and looked down at the pup. "Later, Parker."

"You said earlier you bought Steel to replace Misty. Do you still have her?" Concern the horse might have passed away bothered her. Mallory had ridden Misty many times.

He nodded. "I still have her, but we don't ride as often as we used to. She's in the north pasture right now while I'm working the other horses. I've only had these for about six months so we're still getting used to one another."

Sawyer said to Emma, "Keep a close eye on Maverick. I called Hawk, and he will be watching the ranch. Sammy and Utah will be here, too."

"You know I will."

Sawyer's sister had never liked to be reminded of how to do things, but in this case, Mallory felt the need to explain that her son had never been around large animals. Emma already knew about the two attacks, so she refrained from joining in.

She and Sawyer walked to her truck and got in. "You mentioned Sammy and Utah. I suppose that means Sammy and Owen still work here, but who is Utah?"

He put his buckle on. "Not Owen. That's a long story I can tell you later. Utah is a new farmhand, but he's a fast learner. And yeah, Sammy still works here and is the ranch foreman now that Owen is gone."

It's like she'd forgotten how many people had been a part of Thunder Ridge Ranch. After they pulled out of the drive, the tension in the cab was obvious. She had just left *their* son with his family. It was a big step. Thankfully, he didn't say anything because she didn't want to discuss it at the moment.

"What did you learn about Kari?"

"Most of the files I retrieved today I had already viewed online previously. I was hoping some information had been left out, but it doesn't look like it that I could find." She glanced at him as she pulled out on the road. "I haven't learned much, and there lies the problem. It seemed like the investigator had only asked Kari a few questions, almost like he was checking boxes to say he interviewed people. His girlfriend admitted the last time she'd seen Sam was the night he'd ran off the road. It was almost impossible for Sam to have time to get from Kari's house to Tilda's place and kill three people, put them in the back seat of his truck and drive them out to Dead Man's Curve. It was almost like they didn't want to hear what Kari had to say. They claimed she wasn't a credible witness concerning the timeline since she was his girlfriend. It's like they'd made up their mind that Sam was their killer, and they were just going through the motions of interviews. If something didn't fit the narrative, they moved on."

Sawyer stared at her. "Or maybe the timeline was possible, so they didn't make a priority—" At her glare, he visibly drew a deep breath. "What time did Kari say Sam left her house?"

"Somewhere between six-thirty and seven that night. She had a test in the morning and needed to study, and Sam had gotten up at four-thirty that morning and was going home to get in bed early."

"Okay. We can do a test run later to see if it's possible. Maybe in the morning."

She blinked. "Alright." After a second, she said, "The investigator also asked her if she drove her car out to Dead Man's Curve. Kari denied it."

He looked at her. "Why would they think she did?"

"Because for the police's theory to hold true, Sam needed help getting the bodies in and out of his back seat."

Sawyer finished the thought. "Because moving the bodies would be difficult and take time."

"Exactly." She nodded. "They believed he had an accomplice that helped."

Kari no longer lived in the same house, but twelve miles outside of Cedar Hollow. Mallory wasn't familiar with the street, making her wonder if it was a new subdivision.

"I thought we were meeting her at the Greasy Diner."

"We are." She glanced his way. "But it's only two o'clock and we have a little extra time, so I wanted to see where she lives."

"I hear you. Not often, but sometimes when I'm investigating a case, I do the same thing to get a feel for the person I'm going to interview."

"I remember." There was a lot of things they used to do the same when working as state troopers. She looked at him. "Want to tell me about Brock?"

"Don't go there. Let's just say he's been gone since before Dad died and leave it at that."

"Did he come home for Deacon's funeral? Do you know where Brock's at? Was there some kind of blowup?"

"Little brother is alive. Leave it alone."

Confusion clawed at her. Brock was a few years younger than Sawyer, but he'd always seemed like a good guy when Mallory lived in Cedar Hollow. He was quiet with a sense of humor and spent a lot of time to himself, but still, he had always been friendly. By Sawyer's reaction, she could guess Brock hadn't come back for his dad's funeral. There was something different about Brock—Mallory had always thought he struggled to fit in. Like he had to try too hard. But was that enough to make the youngest Cantrell turn his back on his family? She could only imagine the hurt and anger that had caused everyone.

If Brock didn't come for Deacon's funeral, she couldn't comprehend why. Deacon had made her feel a part of the family from day one. He'd made certain she knew she was welcome for Sunday lunch after church services but also invited her to ride horses on the ranch. He took interest in her job and the cases she'd worked. Mallory's own dad was a decent guy, but he spent a lot of time away from home driving a big rig across the country, sometimes being gone for weeks at time. It'd felt nice for Deacon to step into the role of a father figure, even though she was already an adult. It wasn't just Deacon, but Nora, too. Both of them had included her as soon as Sawyer had brought her to the ranch to meet his family.

Maybe Sawyer would confide in her later about his younger brother.

She eased down the paved street. Three newer, simple brick homes sat in a row. "That's hers. The last one." The ranch-style home looked like it was about sixteen hundred square feet plus a single garage. A cat walked across the porch and jumped into a turquoise-colored rocking chair.

She drove past the home and turned around in the small

circle drive at the end of the road. Once she passed Kari's place again, she picked up her speed.

"What do you think?"

She shrugged. "Nice starter home for someone in her twenties. From what I learned, her husband works as a supervisor at a flour mill over in Shallow Springs."

As she pulled back onto the highway, he asked, "How long have they been married?"

"Three years. She started dating him about six months after Sam died."

Mallory tried to remain relaxed, but she could still feel her body stiffen. She felt ripped off for Sam that everyone simply moved on with their lives, but his ended in a second. *Hc shouldn't havc run from the police.* Thc words came to her unbidden. It was true—he should've let the investigation play out, but she understood why he'd panicked. She only talked to him once in person after the three deaths. He'd still been in the hospital and the police were waiting to talk to him. She advised him not to answer questions until he had a lawyer with him. He had responded, "I have nothing to hide."

The memory still haunted her. She believed his words, but sometimes being interrogated made people nervous and stumble over their words. After reading the transcripts, she understood why investigators aimed their focus on Sam. He kept repeating, "I don't remember what happened." "I don't know how they got in my truck." And then, "I couldn't have done it."

Several minutes later, they pulled outside of the Greasy Diner. The spaces in front of the place were already full. "Let's get this done."

As soon as she entered the diner, she noted the place was three-quarters full. Kari Bryne was sitting at a booth by a window in the middle of the room. Mallory walked over and held out her hand to the woman. "Hello, Kari. Thank you for agreeing to see us."

Kari looked more mature than the kid she was a few years ago in her slacks and silky blouse. Her long black hair that she used to often have pulled into a ponytail was now in a stylish layered bob.

"I don't have a lot of time." Kari glanced around the room at the other patrons.

When Mallory took a seat across from Kari, Sawyer grabbed a chair from a nearby table and placed it on the end, positioning himself between them.

Kari said, "Irving will be home early today, so I'd like be home before then."

"Let's get to it then." Instead of asking her the same questions investigators had previously asked, Mallory went straight to the heart of the matter. "Do you believe Sam killed Phillip and Tilda Pennington and Wilson Newport?"

Kari rubbed her finger on the table in small circles as if in thought. "I don't know."

"What makes you say that?"

She shrugged. "At the time I didn't think Sam could harm anyone. But maybe it was an accident, as in Sam was at Tilda's house for another purpose but then something went wrong or things got heated."

This didn't make sense. "Are you saying you think Sam was having an affair or something with Tilda? I didn't realize they were that close." Mallory had never heard Sam mention Tilda, but she had to assume in a town the size of Cedar Hollow, even if Tilda was three years younger than Sam, they must know each other, even if not well.

"No." Kari shook her head. "Nothing like that."

"What did you mean?"

Kari shrugged. "Maybe the police and townspeople were right. Maybe Sam had broken into their home."

Frustration tugged at Mallory, but she wasn't necessarily surprised. It wasn't uncommon for people's opinions to change over time about the facts. Instead of continuing down that road, she asked, "What about Phillip? Had Sam talked about him? Phillip had moved in with his sister months before to save money from what I understood."

Again, Sam's ex-girlfriend shook her head. "No. Mainly Sam talked about his coworkers at King Roofing. A couple of guys named, uh—" she glanced at ceiling "—Vincent and Trevor, I think."

Mallory nodded to encourage her to keep remembering. "Yeah, his supervisor was Trevor Cain. His boss was a couple of years younger than Sam, but he seemed to be mature for his age."

"Probably." Kari looked at her phone. "Maybe Sam was in the middle of stealing something but was caught."

Mallory refrained from looking at Sawyer. This is what the police believed and continued to repeat. The theft angle had been repeated on the sites Mallory had set up on social media, too. "To your knowledge, had Sam been stealing since you started dating him?"

"Not that I know of. I just don't know what to think. The police found the broken pearl necklace in his console. It's possible." Kari shrugged. "Sam's gone now, and nothing is going to change that."

Mallory schooled her features to hide her irritation. Yes, Sam was gone. He'd get no defense. No trial. Nothing to prove his innocence. Whoever killed three people didn't count on his sister looking into the cold case. "You've had years to think about that night. Is there anything else you've remembered, no matter how inconsequential it seems?"

Kari glanced at her phone, seemingly at the time. "Not really. The situation makes me sad. If he wouldn't have run from the police… If he wasn't guilty, he had nothing to hide. Right?"

That was a favorite comment for people to say when someone was about to be arrested and the suspect panics. Since it was known in town that Sam had stolen before, it was almost certain people would believe him guilty even if he wasn't. "One more. Do you know any of the Jacobsons?"

Kari's face fell. "No, why are you asking that?"

"Curiosity." Kari was Sam's age, so Mallory guessed if Kari knew any of the Jacobson children, it'd be the ones her age. "Are you saying you don't know Randy or Becca?"

"I didn't say that." She shook her head. "I suppose I'm familiar with both of them, but it's not like I talk to them regularly. I really need to go. Irving will be expecting me."

Interesting. "I'm looking into the case again. If you recall anything, please let me know."

"I will." Kari grabbed her phone and small purse.

Mallory was about to get up, when Sawyer asked, "Did you know the Penningtons or the Newports?"

"I've known George and Sally Pennington my whole life." She spoke fast. "It about killed them when both of their children were murdered. I can't even imagine how they felt. I never met Wilson Newport's family."

Sawyer said, "I can't imagine, either."

As they all climbed to their feet, Mallory was only partially satisfied with the meeting, feeling like Kari was just wanting to move on with her life, much like everyone else. "Thanks for meeting with us. You meant the world to Sam, and you were helping him turn his life around. You gave him purpose. I've always appreciated that."

A guilty smile appeared on Kari's lips before she stepped out of the booth. "Sorry I couldn't have been more help."

After Kari scurried out of the diner, Sawyer mumbled, "Laying it on a bit thick, weren't you?"

She turned to him. "Someone needs to. Everyone just wants to move on with their lives. Easy for those who it doesn't affect."

He whispered, "Low blow."

His boots clicked on the concrete floor behind her. As she was about to go out the glass door, an older man with rumpled clothes stepped in front of her, cutting her off. "You have some nerve returning to Cedar Hollow dredging up the past."

All conversations came to a halt in the diner as everyone looked on.

Mallory looked into dark, angry eyes, and it took a moment for her to realize who he was. Travis Newport, Wilson's uncle. The man had aged considerably since the last time she'd seen him. He owned a junkyard and raised Rottweilers on the outskirts of town. He loved to fight, and she wasn't about to engage him in front of noisy townspeople. "Hello, Travis. Excuse me."

When she tried to push past him, his arm shot out and held the door shut. "You're not welcome here. Your dad hightailed it to Florida, and it's about time you run back to wherever you came from."

Someone chimed in, "Yeah."

Sawyer said, "Get out of the lady's way, Travis."

Mallory held up her hand to let Sawyer know his intervention was not needed. "I've got this. I'm sorry for your family's loss, Travis. I'm here on official business with the Texas Rangers. Remove yourself."

Fury burned in the man's eyes and his hand shook. She

continued to stare at him and refused to show emotion. It wasn't easy, but it was something she'd learned, especially over the past five years.

"Fine." Travis dropped his hand, but only moved a few inches back, making it possible to pass by without brushing against him.

All eyes in the diner were on them as she and Sawyer walked out to her truck. She started the engine without a word.

"What do you—"

"What?" she snapped. At his startled expression, she tried to bring down the energy a notch. "Didn't mean to interrupt you. Go ahead."

"What do you think of Kari changing her tune?"

"I didn't like it." The question was annoying because not only did she not learn anything new, but the confrontation with Travis in front of the diner's patrons only added to her frustration. "Did you notice how she didn't like being questioned about knowing Randy and Becca Jacobson?"

"I did." He took off his Stetson and ran his fingers through his hair before returning the hat back on his head. "Where were you going with that?"

Should she explain that it was their mom who contacted her about the missing gun?

"Mallory, I'm on your side." He said the comment with gentleness.

"Then why do I feel like you're just like everyone else in Cedar Hollow? Sam is dead, why not move on?" She imitated Kari's voice, insinuating it was like Sawyer. "Because there's a killer out there who got away with a triple homicide. That person deserves to pay for his crimes."

Being shot at this morning and turning over the tractor had not been in her plans today. And now her first interview hadn't turned up new information. She tried to tame her emotions for she knew it wasn't his fault. Even though she'd arrived only last night, she was feeling the pressure to find new information. It seemed the task of finding someone who was willing to come forward might be more difficult than anticipated.

Sawyer stared at her without a reply. Dressed in her Texas Rangers "uniform" of jeans, boots and a white shirt reminded him of his dad. Mallory had always been confident. If he had to guess, he suspected she was uncertain about this case. It was different back when they used to work with one another because they were with the same department. Now, he wasn't even in law enforcement.

He had to admit he was proud of her for going for her dreams. He also knew this was the biggest case of her life. She was determined to do justice by proving Sam's innocence. No doubt, she had more at stake than anyone else who'd handle the case.

She glanced down at her cell phone. "It's not five yet. I think we have time to go to Dr. Bourg's office. Would you call and check on Maverick?"

The concern in her eyes said she wasn't used to leaving their son with people. He guessed that was a good thing, but it made him wonder. "Besides the babysitter…"

"Evie Clark…"

"Yeah. Besides her, is there anyone else who's been able to help give you a break?"

"No. I've had a couple of women from church offer, but Mav and I make do." Her words came out defensive.

It was probably best he not argue with her. He couldn't fault her for that, but, being from a large, close-knit family, it was hard to imagine not having others around to help.

As she pulled into the clinic, a division of Cedar Hollow Memorial, he put his hand on the door handle.

She hurried to say, “I’ve got this. If you’d be kind enough to wait on me.”

“I don’t mind.”

“I appreciate it, Sawyer. I truly do. But I’d rather do this one on my own.”

He tried not to show his disappointment, but he wished she’d trust him to help. “Dr. Bourg was Tilda’s boss, right?”

She nodded. “Yeah. One of Tilda’s friends, uh, Renae something—a lady she knew from her spin class—had claimed something had been bothering Tilda the week or so before her death. She claimed Tilda said something stressful was going on at work.”

“Okay. Hopefully, you will learn something on this interview.”

“Thanks.” She climbed out of the truck and walked toward the entrance.

Sawyer watched her cross the pavement. She was still just as attractive as the day he’d asked her to marry him. He scrubbed his face with his hand. It was amazing how things could change in an instant. One day they were happy and engaged to be married, and with one phone call from the police telling Mallory her brother had been in an accident, their relationship unraveled.

He guessed he should be thankful he’d learned Mallory wasn’t the sticking kind before they entered into marriage. As soon as the thought crossed his mind, he mentally corrected himself. She never would’ve left him if he’d been more persistent in helping her find the answers she was looking for. He had been satisfied with the results of the investigation, but looking back, it was a mistake to be impatient.

As he stared at the glass door she'd disappeared through, he prayed she'd learn something valuable. He realized that was something that had changed about her. She had asked him to say grace before their meal earlier today and mentioned God several times. Maybe if he would've sought God's help in healing Mallory and for guidance in their relationship, everything might have turned out different.

EIGHT

Mallory entered the single-story building. The beige brick was somewhat out of date, but the paint appeared to be fresh. Green hedges stood under the rectangle glass windows. Even though the clinic was built over sixty years ago and had few renovations, the property was maintained. She went through the glass door, and her boots clicked on the freshly waxed tiled floor.

The hallway led to a door with Dr. Bourg's name. She went in and noted the large lobby filled with modern cushioned chairs. A small fountain stood on the far wall, and two televisions played in opposite corners. She walked up to the receptionist's window.

The woman glanced at her and visibly sighed before she opened a sliding glass window. "Yes?"

"I have an appointment with Dr. Bourg."

"We're closed for the day."

She started to close the window, but Mallory held up her hand. "I'm Texas Ranger Mallory Foster. I scheduled a meeting with the doctor."

The woman's gaze landed on the badge like she had just noticed.

A male voice hollered from a back room, "Send her on back, Lucille. I'm expecting Miss Foster."

Lucille shot her a quick smile. "Go on back."

Mallory walked through a door and down a long, carpeted hallway. Dr. Bourg appeared in the open door. "Come on in."

She followed him inside the quaint office and took a cloth chair across from his desk. She noted the framed degree on the wall and three photos. One included a woman, probably his wife, and another included the woman and a man. Dressed in the same style of clothes, like the pictures were taken at the same time, were the same two people plus another woman and a little boy—Mallory guessed them to be the doctor's daughter-in-law and grandson.

"What can I help you with?" he asked. "Your boy is not having any problem with his arm, is he?"

The man had gray hair and looked to be in decent physical shape. She'd researched him online and learned he was sixty-one and was a member of the Cedar Hollow Memorial Hospital Foundation—a group that not only helped to promote health and wellness in the community, but also raised money for equipment and advances in health care. "Maverick is fine. I wanted to ask you about Tilda Pennington, who worked for you five years ago."

"I remember Miss Pennington." His reading glasses rested on top of his head, and he wore a white coat. "It was a tragedy what happened to her, but I spoke with the police back then. I'm sure if you ask them for their records, they'll let you read my statements."

Even though his words were friendly, she found his tone a tad condescending, but maybe that was the way he always acted. "I'm familiar with the case. What kind of vehicle did you drive five years ago?"

He blinked like he hadn't expected that line of questioning. "I drive a Lexus right now, and let me think..."

Back then I had a BMW. I'm not certain what this has to do with anything."

She ignored his last comment. "One of the other witnesses said Tilda had mentioned she had something bothering her the days leading up to her death. Do you know what that was about?"

"Like I said, I've already answered that question, and my answer is the same. I have no idea what was bothering her or even if something was bothering her. She worked as a receptionist for me for three years."

"Did you know each other outside of work?"

"No. I try to create a good workplace for my employees and treat everyone like family. Tilda was busy with her own life and didn't join in much."

She felt it was important to get the questions out quickly in case he cut their meeting short like Kari had. "Did she mention a boyfriend?"

He shrugged. "Like I said, she didn't join in much with me."

"How many employees did you have at the time?" Mallory got the feeling it annoyed the doctor to answer the questions, but maybe it was because he believed Sam killed her. No doubt he knew Sam was her brother. It was always something she'd have to deal with in Cedar Hollow, but she was determined not to let it deter or shortchange her investigation.

"Two full-time and one part-time. Tilda was my receptionist, and Rosemary Gonzales was my nurse. Maybe Tilda confided in Rosemary. My son was my lab technician. Is that all?" He glanced at the clock on the wall.

She jotted down the information even though there was nothing new that she didn't already know. Normally, she tried to ease into the interview as to not put the interviewee on the defensive, but she could tell that was not going to work. She pivoted. "Not yet. Was Tilda having trouble at work? Have a disagreement with you or the other two employees?"

The doctor frowned. "Tilda got along with everyone. I only have a couple of minutes before I must get ready for my next patient."

Lucille had indicated he was done for the day, but she moved on. "Dr. Bourg, another witness said Tilda was concerned with something going on at work, that she'd come home upset. Why would she say that?"

He sighed. "I didn't want to say anything because it seemed unnecessary to bring it up. Tilda had been caught stealing, and I had to tell her that if it happened again, I'd have to let her go."

That surprised Mallory, but she schooled her features. "When was this?"

"Two or three days before her death. Listen, Miss Foster, I liked Tilda, and she was a good employee. I'm sure she was struggling to pay the bills or something because she had never done anything like this before that we were aware of."

Mallory wasn't certain if she believed his story. "How much money did she take?"

The receptionist rang his desk phone, and Bourg put it on speaker. "Dr. Friedman is on line one."

"Hold on." He pushed the mute button. "I don't recall the amount off the top of my head, but it was over a thousand dollars. Honestly, I've tried to put her senseless murder behind me. Now, I need to take this."

"Wait." Mallory scrambled with this important revelation as questions popped into her head. "How did she steal the money? Was it from credit card fraud from paying patients? Did the office accept cash?"

"Miss Foster, I need to take this call." He dismissed her.

"We need to finish this interview. Thank you for your time." As she got up to leave, she felt his eyes on her back. A few minutes later, she sat in her truck with Sawyer, staring at the clinic.

Dr. Bourg had been friendly enough, but she found it strange he had held back Tilda had been caught embezzling from the company back when the police interviewed him. That was vital information. It's not that Mallory didn't believe people could get themselves in a bind and do something out of character, but she found it strange no one else had ever made a similar complaint. She intended to dig deeper to get to the truth, she told Sawyer.

She turned right on the highway and then took another right at the intersection. Sawyer not responding to her comment made her believe she was on the right track. "I'm not wrong about this."

"You need to find the evidence." He stared at her.

"Yeah. And I will."

"I will help you, Mal." He didn't correct himself this time when he said her name. "Promise me, once you investigate the cold case, no matter what we learn, you will put it in the past once you're through digging."

"I'm going to find who committed the murders."

"Promise me. We have a little boy that depends on us. We can't be the kind of parents we need to be if this continues to hang over our heads. We need to move past this."

"You mean, I need to move past this."

His hand reached across the console and grabbed hers, pulling their grasp between them. "*We* need to get past this. For everyone's sake. I pray that you're right and that Sam was innocent. For your sake and your family's reputation. But if you learn the killer was your brother, can you live with that knowledge?"

Could she handle that? She pulled her hand back and settled it on the steering wheel. Her first thought was yes because she'd been living with the town believing Sam's guilt. But she had never believed her brother was capable of murder. What if he had killed three innocent people? Would she admit it? She was a Texas Ranger and had been in law enforcement for nine years. She'd seen good people fight for the one family member who'd gone astray. Most of the time, their relatives were guilty of a crime or at least a mistake.

Maverick depended on her. He was too young to understand his uncle had been accused of murdering three people. When he got old enough, or he heard it from someone else, how was he supposed to not let it affect the way he looked at their family if Mallory couldn't? She let the way people talk about her mom's drinking affect her. She was barely invited for sleepovers or birthday parties. "I wouldn't like it, but I could live with it."

"Alright, then. Can you do me a favor?"

The way he said it made her think she wouldn't like what he was about to ask. "What is it?"

"Quit putting me in the enemy camp."

She looked at him. His expression said he was serious, but he didn't mean it as an insult. "You're not the enemy."

"Sure?"

She smiled. "Halfway sure."

"At least you're honest." He chuckled.

"Let's get something to eat." She turned into a sandwich joint and pulled up to the drive-through.

"I figured we would eat at the ranch," he said.

"It's not quite dark yet, so I thought we could waste a little time. We'll get something to drink."

He squinted. "What are you up to?"

"Trying to dot all the *i's* and cross the *t's*."

His gaze narrowed, but he didn't say anything more. They sat in the parking lot, taking their time sipping on chocolate shakes and talking about the case. She preferred to keep the topic away from personal matters, so this worked in her favor.

Once they were on their way again and were several miles outside of town, she turned right onto a rock road.

He looked out the window like he'd just realized what road she'd taken. "Really? Why are we going there?"

She wanted to check Dead Man's Curve where Sam's pickup had lost control, sending it along with the three victims into the steep ravine below. The area had been checked for evidence, even by her, but she had to get the feel for what happened that night. A reminder she dreaded. There wasn't a good reason why she wanted to go to the location, so she just told the truth. "I need to see it again."

No matter how hard Sawyer tried to get along with Mallory, he still got the feeling he was getting on her nerves. She was on edge, but that was understandable since she was looking into the murders her brother was blamed for. But Sawyer wasn't against her, and he sincerely hoped that Sam wasn't to blame.

He got out on the passenger side, which was partway in the ditch. He noted she'd parked several feet behind where Sam's Nissan had left the road and entered the ditch. Spring grass had taken over the area. He shut the door and was careful where he stepped. Being late spring snakes should be out and it'd been warm a week or so ago, so he wasn't taking any chances.

Even though the temperatures were in the seventies, Mallory noticeably shivered as she looked out over the steep ravine. Water flowed in the bottom and trees grew up on the banks. He asked, "This would've been the same time of night of the accident?"

She crossed her arms over her chest. "Yeah. Close. It was almost dark when the 9-1-1 call was made. Sam's death had been in April, so daylight savings time had already changed, making it the same as now."

He remembered the date well but didn't reply. Mostly the date stuck with him because it was late May on a Saturday when Mallory broke off their engagement and left the following day so she could start work on Monday. Evidently, she had already applied to transfer to West Texas to be a state trooper in Amarillo before breaking it off with him. That was probably the reason she hadn't even wanted to discuss trying to work their relationship out. She'd already set her plans in order.

For several moments, she stared across the ravine and then back to the ground in front of them. Mallory walked behind her truck and kept walking until she was about thirty yards up the road. Besides the occasional reflection from her badge, she couldn't be seen. Sawyer stayed where he was, giving her time to look without interrupting her thoughts.

A tiny fragment of red glowed from the grass. He bent over and picked it up. The plastic looked like part of a brake light. It could've been from the night of the accident or some other vehicle. Because of the sharp curve, many people had gone over or almost gone over the ravine's edge at this point. After the night of Sam's death, the county replaced the old sign with a new cautionary sharp-curve-ahead sign.

He scouted around but couldn't see much, even though the moon was half full. As Mallory made her way back to him, he moved to the back of her truck. "It a sharp curve and difficult to see, especially at night."

"I know."

"Were his truck's lights on?" he asked.

"Yeah, they were supposed to be when the police got here. There were several tire tracks that night on the side of the road and in the ditch. Also that tree," she pointed, "had an indention and missing bark like it had been hit. I think someone else was here that night."

As he glanced over the ravine's edge, he thought about how Mallory had questioned the seemingly too many tracks and the mark on the trunk. "That's about thirty feet."

"Thirty-four feet," she corrected him.

"If your theory is correct," he continued, "and someone else was here, what do you think they were doing?"

"Disposing of the bodies. Sam might have lost control and hit that tree. The impact could've been from the tree and not slamming into the bottom of the ravine. It would remain consistent with the concussion. Then the killer could've moved the bodies from his or her vehicle into Sam's truck. It's a long shot, I know. I'm not saying that's how it happened. Just thinking of the possibilities."

Sawyer added, "Maybe the real killer was the one to make that call."

She glanced at him. "Sometimes you surprise me, cowboy."

Mallory had always been a good law officer and had a good head on her shoulders. He'd always believed she was blinded by love for her brother, but he couldn't discount her savvy, either. Headlights came at them from the way they had approached the curve. Thirty seconds later, an SUV passed, not hitting their brake until they were right on Mallory's vehicle.

"Told you." She stepped to the ravine's edge and glanced over again. "It's hard to see here."

"I agree. It is a dangerous curve. Hard to believe the county still hasn't put up guardrails to keep vehicles from driving over the edge even though countless people had been injured over the years."

"I know. I remember Belinda Donley went over right after she'd gotten her driver's license."

Sawyer nodded. "I remember that, too. What was the weather like that night? Clear?"

She nodded toward her truck. He followed her cue, and they climbed back in. She said, "Partly cloudy. No rain or fog. Fifty-eight degrees."

"Sticking to your theory. If the killer was out here, where could he or she have parked their vehicle where it couldn't have been seen?"

"Anywhere. Maybe it was in the middle of the curve and that's what made Sam hit the tree."

"Someone would have to be strong to move three bodies. Wilson Newport was a big guy, over six feet and over two-twenty-pounds."

"Yep. Sam weighed one-seventy, but Wilson would be a lot for him to handle by himself." She put the truck into Drive and pulled out on the road. About a half mile up the road, she turned the vehicle around at an intersection.

"The police's conclusion is that Sam killed the three people, put them in his truck, drove them out here with plans to drive them into the ravine. If he was planning to dump them into the ravine, wouldn't he have slowed down? Why go so fast that he lost control?" Even as he asked the question, he knew the answer. The police thought his nerves were shot after killing three people.

"Like I said, I believe he hit that tree and was framed. There were too many tracks on the side of road. It had rained two days before then, so they were fresh. I don't know who or exactly how the killer pulled it off, but he did." For the first time since the murders happened, the police's theory seemed to have holes. "It's possible, but definitely not likely, especially if you take the time Kari claims Sam left her house."

She gave him a big nod. "Exactly."

If Mallory was right and Sam was framed, then someone had killed three people and was still on the loose. That gave them great motivation to try to stop her and the Texas Rangers from solving the case. And that meant the attacks would only grow worse.

NINE

Even though Sawyer didn't say it out loud, Mallory believed he was starting to see the holes in the case against Sam. Interviewing Kari and visiting Dead Man's Curve had helped Mallory get her mind into an investigative mode. But the threat to her and Maverick were never far away.

As if Sawyer's thoughts were along the same path, he talked into his cell phone. "How is Maverick?" He nodded as he listened. "We're on our way home. Will be there shortly."

Home. The word wasn't lost on Mallory. It was Sawyer's and the other Cantrell family member's home. Not hers. She asked, "Everything good?"

"Yeah. They're trying to bribe Maverick to come into the house." He smiled. "They've had no suspicious activity."

"I know things aren't exactly smooth between us, but I want you to know I appreciate your family stepping up and helping us."

He cocked his head at her. "You knew they would, Mal."

He was right. Yes, his family had been rallying the troops. If one person needed help, they all came running. It could be a good and a bad thing depending on the perspective. "Still. I wanted you to know."

In the light from the instrument panel, she could see him staring at her.

"I want to tell Maverick the truth."

She let the words percolate. She wanted to put it off, but she didn't know exactly why. Was she hoping her son wouldn't have to find out? "Wouldn't it be easier once this case is closed, and we can give him the time he needs to adjust?"

"Are you planning on staying in Cedar Hollow after you're through with your investigation?"

Headlights pulled onto the highway from behind them. "No. Maybe a couple of days, but I wasn't planning on taking vacation."

"Don't you think it's important I get to spend time with him as his dad? I sure do." His voice rose a smidgeon.

She didn't blame Sawyer, but in her mind, she still saw him as the person who didn't want anything to do with their child. It wasn't true, she knew that now, but over four years of believing that made it difficult to absorb the change. She needed to be fair. "I agree. It's important."

He laughed, but not in a nice way. "Good. I don't want to fight you on this, Mallory. I want to work together to do what's right for our son."

"I'm glad to hear you say that." In her rearview mirror, the vehicle drew closer. Its headlights were on bright beams. A check to her speedometer said she was going the speed limit. She maneuvered closer to the white line to make certain she gave the vehicle plenty of room to pass if it wanted to. "Come on around."

Sawyer looked over his shoulder and then pulled out his gun. "I wish I knew if that's what the guy who tried to take Maverick was driving."

"Me, too." She slightly pressed on the accelerator, easing the speed upward.

The silver Tahoe SUV pulled into the other lane to pass, then pulled along beside her. She glanced over her shoulder to get a look at the driver. Only a dark silhouette could be seen.

Something hit her dash, and her rearview mirror exploded. A bullet hole showed in the middle of her windshield.

She slammed on her brakes, momentarily startled.

"Shooter on the right," Sawyer yelled. "Keep going."

"The right?" She let off the brake and hit the gas again, trying to stay in her lane. "Are you hurt?"

The Tahoe had taken off with only his taillights showing in the distance.

"Negative," he said as he looked back over his shoulder.

Pieces of glass from the broken rearview mirror lay across her dash and splattered over her seat and floorboard. Finally, she pulled onto the shoulder of the road. "Did you see who shot at us? Was it another vehicle?"

He shook his head. "I didn't see a vehicle. It happened so fast. Are you okay?"

"Yeah."

"Then get us to the ranch. That was a setup."

Her hands trembled, and she kept a tight grip on the wheel so that Sawyer wouldn't see. "I'm confused. Where did the shot come from?"

"Someone was waiting for us to pass at Wagon Rut Road. Hold on." Sawyer quickly hit a number on his cell phone. The name Hawk glowed on the screen.

"I'm turning around," she announced. Sawyer quickly told his brother about the shooting and let him know their location.

She wasn't about to let someone shoot at them without trying to see who it was. Taking the next turn, she sped down Brodrick Lane and then took the first right, trying to come up behind the person who'd shot at them. "No vehicle?" she asked again.

"I'm not certain, but it seems like the SUV and the person were working together."

She nodded. "I was thinking the same thing." At Wagon Rut Road, she turned right but kept her speed down. It was a white rock road. As they neared the intersection with the highway, she turned off her headlights and then continued at a slow pace.

"I see taillights." Sawyer pointed. "Looks like a motorcycle."

She thought he was right as she approached. Sure enough, it was a green motorcycle. She stopped the truck, put it into Park and pulled out her service weapon. "Let's see who's shooting at us."

As she stepped out on the rocky road, she heard Sawyer's boots on the gravel. The guy on the motorcycle was sitting on the bike with the engine idling. So far, he hadn't turned around or indicated he knew they were there. As she approached, she realized the guy was talking on his phone using Bluetooth.

She met Sawyer's gaze and nodded, indicating she was approaching the cyclist. She kept to the guy's left. Twenty feet away. Fifteen. Ten. "Texas Ranger. Step off the motorcycle with your hands up."

Visibly the man jumped before jerking around to look at her. His long auburn hair and helmet kept most of his face hidden. Instead of doing as she said, he hit the gas and took off, making the back tire fishtail.

She shot off two rounds. The guy leaned forward and

grabbed his shoulder before disappearing down the highway. She and Sawyer hurried back to her truck. They took off and turned right on the highway in the same direction the motorcycle had gone.

"You'll never catch him," Sawyer said. "I think that's the same green motorcycle I'd seen earlier. Looked like a Kawasaki Ninja."

"I know I can't catch him. That would be my guess on the type also." She eased off the accelerator and rubbed the back of her neck. "I'm convinced that was planned with the driver of the Tahoe. I'm thankful the guy's aim was off."

As the lines whizzed by on the highway, she had the urge to hurry back to Maverick. "These guys don't seem to be professional hitmen."

"I had the same thought. But they're not playing around."

"You mean like they're not just trying to warn me away from the case but would be okay if I was dead."

His brown eyes connected with hers. "Something like that."

For Sawyer to agree with her only made any morsel of doubt of Sam's guilt vanish. Her brother was innocent, and that meant a killer was out there that had no choice but to eliminate her. Even though she had been attacked multiple times, this last attempt made her realize it would only take one mistake on her part, or a lucky aim from one of the subjects, to end this investigation for good.

By the time they arrived at the ranch, Sawyer was certain he needed to do more to keep her safe. Hawk needed to be with them when they went somewhere. But that also meant there'd be one less person to keep an eye on Maverick.

Mallory pulled around the back of the house and parked

behind Hawk's truck. Emma stepped out from the barn and motioned them over.

"I hope everything is okay," Mallory muttered as she scrambled from the vehicle.

Sawyer hurried to the barn with his hand on his weapon, ready for what might await them.

The lights hanging from the rafters illuminated the stalls and the stack of square bales below. His son wasn't in sight. "Where is Maverick?"

Emma glanced up and then her mouth fell open. She pointed at his gun. "Put that away."

He allowed his hand to fall to his side and noticed Mallory had done the same. "What's going on?"

Emma smiled and waved at Mallory. "Come here. I want you to see this."

Sawyer stepped up to the stall and glanced down. Maverick was curled up next to a newborn calf, both of them sound asleep.

"Ooh," Mallory murmured. She took her cell phone from her pocket and clicked several photos. "That's the most precious thing."

Emma put her hand to her chest. "I know. I tried to get him to come in before it got dark, but he kept asking for one more minute. The calf laid down at his feet and went to sleep, and Mav laid beside and pet him until he, too, went out."

"Is Hawk around?"

"Yes, big brother, Hawk and Cash have been in and out of the barn multiple times." Emma shook her head like Sawyer should know better than to question their safety. "Mom and Shaylee spent time out here, too. No one is getting close to that boy unless they go through at least five people."

Mallory stepped inside the stall and picked Maverick up

in her arms. The boy barely moved as he laid his head on her shoulder. The scene gave Sawyer an ache in his chest. It was easy to see how much she cared for their son. It was in Sawyer to take Maverick from her because he was a little big for her to be carrying, but he realized it was something Mallory wanted to do.

"I'll see y'all in the house," Sawyer whispered. As he was walking away, he heard Maverick utter, "Can I sleep out here?"

Mallory answered, "You can visit the animals again tomorrow."

When Sawyer stepped outside, Hawk was headed toward him from the main house.

His brother said, "Everything's been quiet. You want to give me an update?"

"Sure. Let's go inside because I'm starving." Covered dishes sat on the dining table. He lifted the lids to meat loaf in one and mashed potatoes in another. Even though they had shakes at the drive-through, he hadn't eaten much.

"Let me warm you up a plate," Shaylee said, coming into the kitchen from the living room.

Sawyer could do it himself, but hc thought Shaylee enjoyed waiting on them when there were visitors like Mallory and Maverick in the house. "Thanks. I'm sure Mallory will want something, too."

"Two plates coming up."

Hawk glanced in the direction of the cook and took a seat at the table. "I've been keeping an eye on the security cameras and listening to the police scanners. I assume you called Sheriff Copeland to tell him about the shooting."

"I reported in afterward, but Mallory is a Texas Ranger."

"I'm aware." Hawk cleared his throat. "Tell me the location and the description of the vehicles again."

Mallory walked through the door carrying Maverick, and Emma was right behind her with Parker.

Shaylee said, "I'm warming a plate of food for you. I put a helping of everything on there. Hope that's okay."

"It smells wonderful. I'm going to give Maverick a bath and get him ready for bed since he's already eaten."

Sawyer climbed to his feet. "I'm going to see if Mallory needs any help. I'll be right back, and we can finish this conversation."

Hawk and the others watched him as he left the room. Sawyer didn't care. Let them all stare. He wanted to help put his son to bed. When he got to the top of the stairs, he heard Mallory running water in the tub in his bathroom.

"Hey, little guy." Sawyer scrubbed him on the head. "How did you like the animals?"

Mav's eyes grew. "I got to pet the horse and baby cow. Emma helped me feed it with a bottle. The calf hit me with his head, but I was strong." He held up his arm and showed him his bicep.

Sawyer chuckled and gave his arm a squeeze. "Look at that. You *are* strong. You're going to make a great cowboy someday."

"Yeah. And then I can ride the horse."

As Sawyer nodded, he caught Mallory looking at Maverick with a wistful smile, but she turned her gaze on him.

"We will be going home," she mouthed.

"I know." That was all he needed to say. He didn't like it, but she was right. As much as he wanted Maverick to have the time of his life, Mallory and Maverick would be going back west in a few days. He didn't want to make it any harder on the boy than necessary.

What was he saying? It'd be even harder on Sawyer to let him go. He didn't want to be a part-time dad.

Later, after Mallory and Sawyer had eaten dinner and he had discussed the shooting on the highway with Hawk and relayed his description of the SUV and motorcycle, it was past ten o'clock.

Hawk said, "I know you're worried about this, Sawyer, but there's no safer place than the ranch."

Mallory had gone upstairs to go to bed in his room with Maverick. The others, except for Hawk and Cash, also turned in. Cash was working in the office in the barn. Utah and Sammy, the farmhands, stayed in the attached bunkhouse of the barn.

"I know that. We need to find out who killed Tilda and Phillip Pennington and Wilson Newport. At least then we could find the people connected to the person and bring them down." There was plenty of protection at the ranch, so why did he feel like they were vulnerable?

He recalled the image of Mallory holding Maverick, and he had his answer. Because so much was at stake. Not just the safety of his son, but he was beginning to dread the thought of Mallory being out of his life again.

TEN

As Mallory lay in bed, she thought about everything she had been through since arriving in Cedar Hollow. Danger was always a possibility in her line of work, but honestly, most days were uneventful, with time spent chasing down information and talking with people. Only occasionally did she feel like she was in a dangerous situation.

Sawyer had been more helpful than she'd anticipated, especially given the way things had ended.

The night she had broken up with him, he had once again mentioned she needed to face the evidence that her brother was guilty. She remembered exactly where she was like it was yesterday. They were at Thunder Ridge Ranch, standing beside his truck, and he was wearing the royal blue Western shirt she'd bought him for Christmas. Being that it was two days after her mama's funeral and her dad had left the day before in his semi, she had gone to his home for a meal of fried chicken, gravy and biscuits that Nora had made. After they walked outside, they began to argue about the case.

"You need to let this go. It's destroying you. You just buried your mama. I worry about you. We'll never have a future until you let it go."

"We'll never have a future?" Her voice grew loud. "You

know, I think you're right." She tossed the chicken leg she was holding onto the paper plate, sending it off of the plate and onto the ground.

"Mal, don't get so mad. I'm on your side. I don't blame you for defending your brother, but you have blinders on. It's time to look at the evidence and put your feelings aside. For us."

"I've done nothing but follow the evidence. It doesn't add up." She shook her head, feeling nothing but disgust. "How could I have ever considered marrying you? I thought you were on my side."

"I *am* on your side." He attempted to take her hand into his, but she jerked it away.

"This is not a minor issue that I can walk away from. The wedding is off. I can't marry you. I need someone who will stand by me. All I wanted was to *thoroughly* look into my brother's case. He didn't kill those people. He had over twenty-three hundred dollars in his bank account. That's more money than he ever had. Sam didn't break into Tilda's house to steal."

"I do stand by you. That's why I need you to face the truth. The police have quit investigating."

She planted her hands on her hips. Anger and hurt had boiled through her veins. She was still grieving Sam's death, and her mom drank herself to death. Her dad had been spending more time on the road. Sawyer was the one person she thought she could depend on. She stared into his brown eyes, internally pleading for him to wrap his arms around her and tell her she should keep looking into the case until she was satisfied. Crickets chirped in the night as the silence between them dragged out. The knife in her heart twisted.

She'd been wrong. "Take me home."

"Don't do this, Mal."

"Take me home, now. I have nothing more to say."

All the way home, he tried to talk to her, but she couldn't get the words out for fear of bursting into tears. She had waited for him to offer to help her investigate Sam's case. For any sign of hope that he believed it was possible her brother was innocent. But he refused to admit there was even a minute chance.

The last thing he'd said to her before she got into her truck that night was, "Think it over. In the morning, you'll see this differently."

But that night, she had packed a bag and made plans to go to the panhandle of West Texas. She'd already searched for job opportunities and had applied for a transfer for an opening in Amarillo.

The memory still brought sadness to her. It'd been the biggest argument they'd ever had, but it had been coming for several weeks after her brother's death. The more the police department wanted to close the books on the case, the more Sawyer argued she needed to move on.

Now, years later, he acknowledged that Sam was probably innocent, but it didn't bring her the satisfaction she'd dreamed about. It took forever for her to fall asleep.

The next morning after breakfast, Mallory went over her notes and made plans before she went outside to spend a little time with Maverick. They would only be safe when the true killers were behind bars, but she also found it necessary to make time for Maverick after the attempted abduction the other day. So far, the event didn't seem to have too much negative effect, but she believed that was due to the ranch and being around the animals, which diverted his attention.

From upstairs, she watched from the window as Maverick walked behind his dad with an armful of hay in his hands. They stopped in front of Duchess, and Sawyer scooped Maverick into his arms and held him up until he dropped the feed over the rail. The palomino nodded her head as she munched on the hay.

She clasped her hands to her chest. The sight was what she'd pictured her life would be five years ago when she was planning her future with Sawyer. They would both work in law enforcement but spend their free time on the ranch. He'd talked about buying their own place somewhere close to here—remaining close to family, but not too close. Many nights as she lay in bed staring at the ceiling, she would dream of how things could've been if the Cedar Hollow murders hadn't happened.

Learning she was expecting Maverick had been a shock. She'd left Cedar Hollow and had started her new job and moved into an apartment. During her second week on the job, she started feeling queasy in the mornings. Things had been so busy, the cause didn't occur to her until several weeks later. Getting pregnant out of wedlock had not been in her plans, and it spurred her into making life-changing decisions. First, she was going to be the best mom she could be, and to do that, she needed God on her side. She'd not grown up going to church. She began praying and studying the Bible. It wasn't long before she began attending worship services.

However, her anger and hurt at Sawyer had festered since she left. To say his lack of response to the three texts she had sent him in one week to let him know they were going to have a baby was hurtful was an understatement. In the back of her mind, she envisioned him traveling to Amarillo, hoping to work out their relationship, maybe reconciling and raising their son together. But that didn't happen. If it hadn't been for Peggy Adams, an older lady with uncanny wisdom she'd met at church, she might not have mailed Sawyer an envelope with Maverick's newborn pictures. Not wanting the letter to be intercepted by his family, she'd addressed it to Sawyer in care of the Texas Department of Public Safety. She still didn't know what happened to that letter. Back when she worked there, it was Steven McDonald who passed out the mail. At this point, it wouldn't do any good to seek an answer to the question, so she decided to let it drop.

Mollie Beth ran along beside Maverick and Sawyer as they disappeared into the barn. She hated the thought of taking Maverick away from here. He looked so happy, and Sawyer was good to him. No matter how much Mallory had tried her best by her son, he would benefit by having his dad in the picture.

After an early lunch, she, Sawyer and Maverick headed to town to interview Wilson Newport's parents. After much discussion, she and Sawyer had agreed to take Maverick with them. Hawk was busy running down a couple of leads, while Cash was trying to find the identity of the drivers of the vehicles after last night's shooting. There wasn't much to go on, but if anyone could find the information it was Cash.

"You know there's a good chance Lewis and Evelynn Newport won't speak with you." Sawyer looked at her. "Understandably, the couple took it hard when Wilson was killed. They've withdrawn from the community."

"Even though I don't live here anymore, I realize that's more than a possibility. It's not uncommon for family to take out their frustrations on law enforcement." It was more than her being an officer, for it was wildly accepted Sam killed them. After Travis's outburst at the diner, she was under no illusions the family would try to help. "You can never tell what information you can gather, even when the people are not trying to help."

"I have a stop before we go by Wilson's parents."

His eyebrows shot up in question. "Well?"

"I'm going by Janet Jacobson's place of work. It's on the way, and I'm hoping it will provide us a lead."

"You never did tell me why you asked Kari about the Jacobsons."

"I know." She let out a breath. "It was Janet Jacobson who sent me the anonymous email telling me about the missing gun. I need to visit with her. She must have believed it was credible information but didn't want me to know who sent it. It makes me think it's because she doesn't want to be involved or is scared to come forward. Being that the Smith and Wesson is missing from the evidence room means she could be right. I'm hoping she will tell me how she learned it."

He worked his jaw. "You're thinking she heard it from one of her kids?"

"Possibly. Do you know the family very well?"

He nodded. "Mainly Randy. He's been in and out of trouble from what I remember."

"Yeah. He's married twice, and the second wife filed a restraining order against him. He ignored the order and broke three of the wife's ribs. That landed him in county for three months."

"You think Randy took the gun?"

"It's worth looking into. And I believe Kari knows something more. We'll find out after I set up an interview with Janet." She pulled up to Frank's Five and Dime store. "I'll be right back."

She hurried through the glass door, and a bell rang. A

soda fountain lined the far wall, and a variety of goods were displayed on shelves.

"May I help you?"

Mallory was disappointed as she stepped up to the counter to see the person standing behind the register was a younger woman. "Is Janet working today?"

The woman's large blue earrings trembled as she shook her head no. "I'm sorry. Janet's still on vacation, but she should be back on Monday. Is there anything I can help you with?"

"I appreciate it." She started to hand her a business card, but Janet had been careful to hide her identity. "That's okay. I was in town and thought I'd drop by. I'll catch her some other time." She grabbed three old-fashioned cherry candy sticks and handed them to the clerk. She paid and hurried back outside to the truck.

Sawyer looked at her expectedly.

"Janet is on vacation. I may drop by her house later in case she didn't go out of town." She unwrapped one of the pieces of candy and handed it over the back seat to Maverick.

"Yay." He quickly shoved it in his mouth.

"What do you say?"

"Thank you."

Hearing Maverick's sweet voice always brought her joy. A few minutes later, she pulled up to Wilson Newport's parents' small brick house and then turned to look at Maverick. "Mama will be right back. Sawyer is going to stay with you."

"Are we going to get ice cream?" Her son directed the question at Sawyer.

The cowboy smiled. "Probably not today. We'll be going back to the ranch when we're done here."

"I can see the horses and cows again?"

"You sure can." Sawyer turned his attention back to her. "Are you certain you don't want me to be the one to talk with them? I don't mind."

If she thought the Newports were going to react kindly to her visit, she would've asked Sawyer and Maverick to come in. Even though Maverick might be a good buffer, she couldn't take the chance. Sawyer had been close to Phillip, and being that Phillip hung out with Wilson, he might also be the best one to interview them. "I appreciate the offer, but I'd rather be the one. It's my case."

"Okay. We'll be right here."

She climbed out of the vehicle and two huge dogs ran out from behind the house, barking up a storm. She held her hand out for them to sniff, "Hey, doggies. I'm not going to hurt you."

The animals looked like they were part Saint Bernard but were more washed out in color. Probably mixed with a Great Pyrenees. Typically, those breeds were friendly. The larger one stopped about ten feet away, but the other with a solid white face kept coming.

"Get out of here!" Sawyer had gotten out of the truck and was waving his arms.

The dog with the white face ignored Sawyer and snapped at her. "I'm getting back inside the truck," Mallory said.

She and Sawyer climbed in the vehicle while the dogs kept barking. "Maybe I'll come back later."

Suddenly all grew quiet. She looked up to see Lewis Newport on the porch. The dogs ran back to him with their tails wagging.

She stepped back out and called out, "May I speak with you?"

The older man squinted. "You Mallory Foster?"

"Yes, sir."

"Nope, you may not. I have nothing to say to you."

"Would you put your dogs away?" She took a few steps forward but kept a leery eye on the dogs. "The Texas Rangers have reopened the case involving your son's homicide."

"No need to. As long as I tell them to leave you alone, the dogs will obey."

That didn't sound like a friendly invitation, but surely even Mr. Newport wouldn't allow his animals to attack her. "I won't take much of your time."

Lewis let her make it all the way to the steps before he repeated, "I have nothing to say to you. Your brother killed my son. I owe you nothing."

She needed to deescalate the situation. "After finding some new information, the Rangers want to look at the case again."

"Listen, lady. You're not hearing me." He looked at her from over his glasses. "Sam Foster destroyed our family. The missus is living off of antidepressants, and our other son is sitting in a jail cell somewhere in Timbuktu, Louisiana. Now get off of my land."

Normally, she would get more assertive, but she didn't believe it would be wise, especially with Maverick sitting in the truck. Were the man to sic his dogs on her, it would scare her son good. "Fine." She put her hand in the air. "I'll be in town for the next few days. You can call Cantrell Security and Investigations if you want to get ahold of me."

She'd no more turned around than yelling came from inside the house, and a door slammed.

"What is *she* doing here?" The question had a couple of colorful descriptions tossed in.

Mallory turned long enough to see Evelynn Newport storm onto the porch. She'd lost weight, and her eyes looked hollow since the last time she'd seen her. This had been a mistake. She'd have to gather information from other family members.

Either Lewis commanded the dogs to attack, or Evelynn's yelling did the trick, but they rushed to Mallory's heels in a barking and snapping frenzy. She normally wasn't nervous of dogs, but the white face dog's teeth came so close to her ankle, she could feel his breath. Her heart was pounding in her ears by the time she slammed the door on the truck.

She started the engine and pulled out without saying a word.

"Those dogs weren't nice," Maverick observed as he leaned over to look at them from the back seat. "Did they bite you?"

"No, honey, they didn't. Mama is fine." She couldn't help herself but to glance at Sawyer as she turned onto the road. His jaw twitched, which she recognized as him trying to control his anger.

"That was nonsense," he said flatly. He picked up her hand and kissed it. "Are you certain you're okay?"

"I already said I was." She put her hand back on the steering wheel like he hadn't kissed it. "Sawyer, I'm fine. I wouldn't have let them hurt me." He didn't respond, but she could feel his eyes on her like he was saying she had to be kidding. She sighed, ready to put the moment behind her. Progress couldn't be slowed because the Newport family was still grieving. "Maybe Bo will help me."

"Wilson's brother?"

She turned onto the highway toward the ranch. "Yeah. Why do you say it like that? He was close to my age. He was a decent guy."

Sawyer said, "Let Cash or Hawk go see Bo. I don't like

you seeing the victims' families. It's like they're daring you to approach them. They'd like nothing more than for you to give them a reason to let their frustrations out on you."

"I'll not be run off for doing my job. I didn't become a Texas Ranger by avoiding difficult situations or people." Irritation crawled over her. Mainly because she had been nervous at the Newport house. She could've used a weapon to fight against the animals, but it wasn't their fault the owner trained them to be that way. To hear him voice it out loud didn't help her calm her nerves.

"That's not what I was saying." His voice showed its own frustration. "I'm concerned about you, Mallory. And Maverick."

She released a breath. He was right. "Alright. I'll let your brothers visit Bo, but I call the shots. I don't want anyone to take over my investigation. I'm not going to let anything happen to me or Maverick."

Bam!

A red GMC pickup had run through a stop sign and hit her truck on the driver's side, knocking her truck into a utility pole on the side of the intersection.

Her head jerked to the right and bounced back into the driver's side window.

The passenger side of her truck was pressed against the wooden pole. Maverick screamed, causing her to reach back to see if he was alright.

The driver got out of the red pickup and pointed a gun at Sawyer while the passenger scrambled out and ripped open the back door of her truck. He unbuckled Maverick.

Mallory tried to get out, but the GMC's bumper was penned against her door.

Sawyer aimed his gun at the driver, but the passenger made certain he kept Maverick in his line of sight.

The driver scurried into his vehicle with Maverick, and the GMC backed up. The tires squealed as it took off going east.

"Go, go! We can't let them get away."

She hit the gas, and her truck squeaked but ran. Her door was smashed, and probably the wheel fender, but there wasn't any damage to the engine. Her neck throbbed from the whiplash, but she was barely aware of the pain as she sped down the highway. "He ran that stop sign on purpose and pinned your side against the truck on purpose," her voice came out loud. "Didn't he?"

"It would be a chancy maneuver, but yeah, it looks like it. Do you want me to drive?"

"I'm driving." She glared at him. She knew he was as anxious as she was to get Maverick back before the kidnappers got away, but she didn't want to discuss who'd be the better driver. As Sawyer called one of his brothers, she hugged the curves and tried not to let the GMC get out of sight. The damage to her truck didn't seem to inhibit it in any way.

What did they want with Maverick? He was just a little boy and had to be scared to death. Her heart hurt as she thought about him wondering where she was. As fast as she was traveling, the other vehicle could barely be seen. Being early afternoon the traffic was light, which was the only thing they had going for them.

Please, Lord, help me to get my boy back before the kidnappers can get away. She doubted they had buckled him in. *And please help them not have an accident with Maverick in their truck.*

Sawyer quickly relayed to Hawk what had happened and which way they were headed. After several miles, they still had not gained on the kidnappers. He had not meant to insult Mallory with the request to drive, and he was glad she'd turned him down. As it was, they had stayed about the same distance behind the pickup, which may have kept them from having a wreck. Anger and shock burned through him. Who would take a four-year-old boy?

After another fifteen minutes passed, he texted Hawk to give him an update on his location.

Sawyer asked, "Do you have plenty of gas?"

"Yes. I filled up yesterday." Her neck and posture were stiff as both of her hands gripped the steering wheel. The road turned into a jumble of hills and curves. "Where do you think they're taking him?"

"I'm not sure. Lake Kendrick is out this way, but it's been years since I've been there."

She nodded. "I've been there once when I was about ten or twelve."

He tried to pull up GPS on his phone, but he only had one bar, causing it to buffer. "Signal is spotty out here."

"I wonder if that's why they chose this location."

He said, "Could be. Or maybe they have a cabin or something out here." Of course, the kidnappers could keep going another hour or two and be in Louisiana, or head north to Arkansas. He chose not to mention that out loud.

"Do you see them?" She sounded concerned.

He held his breath and looked. "There."

The GMC had turned onto a red dirt road. A huge dust cloud bellowed behind them.

"They're flying. I hope they don't wreck." Mallory turned onto the road. "What do you think their plans are?"

He knew what she was asking. She wanted to know if they planned to hurt him. "I've wondered the same thing.

I doubt they are wanting to hurt him because they could've already done that without driving this far."

"I was thinking the same thing. Not unless they wanted to make me pay. Kind of like if the kidnapper is from the Pennington or Newport family and they want to make me suffer like they've suffered."

The concern in her eyes tore at his heart. He said, "We're going to rescue our son. I won't let them do anything like that."

"Okay." She didn't sound convinced. "I've lost them again."

"Slow down." He looked out of the windows, searching for where the GMC could've gone. There were very few roads out here, and the forest was thick with foliage and towering pine trees.

"I don't see the dust cloud anymore, but the road is filled with more potholes, so maybe they had to slow down."

"I'm certain we haven't lost them. If they pulled off, we'll find them even if we have to drive down every road." He pointed. "There's a driveway."

She pulled down the dirt drive and snaked around until it ended at a circle drive. There were no vehicles or structures in sight. "I don't think this is it."

"Me, either. There was a pile of rocks in a circle like someone had used the place for a campfire in the past. Turn around. Most of this land goes for cheap prices since it's difficult to get water and electricity out here."

She pulled back out on the road and leaned forward in the seat. He found himself doing the same thing, leaning forward and his hand was planted on the dash as he searched for the kidnappers. A couple of minutes crawled by as they eased up the road. His muscles grew more tense as concern grew.

Tears formed in her eyes. "What if we lost him?"

"We didn't." He looked at her and placed his hand on hers. "We just need to keep searching." He couldn't let his mind go there. He let go of her hand and glanced at his phone. It showed they were not getting cell signal. If he could tell Hawk where they were, they could have more people on the search. Hopefully his brothers could figure out the general direction they'd gone. A fallen tree took up half the road and Mallory drove around it. On the other side was another narrow path. "Take that one."

"I see it." She pulled in.

The ground went downhill at a sharp incline through a maze of pine trees. After a couple of hundred yards, a tent appeared among the trees. Fishing poles leaned against a tree, an ice chest was set outside the tent, and three folding chairs—one of them child sized—were placed near a campfire ring of rocks.

"Looks like someone is staying here," she said. A frown enveloped her face as she looked ahead. "That's the kidnappers' vehicle up ahead."

Sure enough, the older model GMC with a bent front bumper was parked along the trail and the green Kawaski motorcycle beside it. She pulled to a stop close to the campsite. "Let's go."

After they got out, she said, "Do you have plenty of ammunition?"

"I do. I have an extra clip."

"I have two service weapons." She headed down the hill with her gun in hand. "You know this might be a trap. I didn't follow closely on the road, but I'm certain they knew we were back there."

"I agree, but I'm going to get my boy." They swiftly hiked down the trail beside each other, but both were wary.

Except for the trail, the area was thick in foliage. He looked in the big GMC's window. "There's no one inside." Not that he thought there would be.

As they headed deeper into the woods, he kept a watchful eye on the trees for movement. Besides a squirrel and the limbs gently blowing in the breeze, all was still. Only the cushioned sound of them walking across the pine needles could be heard.

A few more yards and a faint hum sounded in the distance. At first, he wasn't certain of the source, but as they drew closer, he realized it was running water.

She looked over her shoulder and whispered, "That's a creek or river."

"I think the Copperhead River is in the area." To his remembrance it was decently wide, but not deep. There had been a decent amount of rain this spring.

Brush overtook the trail, forcing them to go through the dense foliage, and the sound of the rushing water grew. Sawyer had tried to prepare himself for different scenarios that they might come upon, but what he saw in front of them shocked him.

Mallory gasped and her steps faltered.

Maverick was sitting in a blow-up boat in the middle of the fast-moving water. The boat was tied to a rock with a rope, keeping it from floating away. At least for now.

"Mom!" Maverick screamed. "Help me!"

"I'll get him," Sawyer said. But he and Mallory hurried into the water at the same time. The current tugged at his boots, even though he was only knee-deep. As he rushed deeper into the river, he glanced around for the kidnappers but didn't see them.

Whatever the men had planned, it had worked. He was willing to do anything to save his son. Mallory fought the current right beside him. Love for their son was one thing they both had in common. He prayed it didn't cost them their lives.

ELEVEN

Mallory could barely breathe as she maneuvered through the rushing water. Maverick watched her approach and held his hands out to her, tears in his eyes and his mouth turned into a frown. The boat bounced up and down with the current. "Hold on, I'm almost there."

Sawyer got there first and caught hold of the back of the boat in an attempt to hold it still.

When she grabbed the edge, she noticed a small belt-like strap wrapped around Maverick's waist securing him in the center of boat. His feet were tied together, but his hands were free. Her heart broke at how pathetic he looked. How could someone do this to a child?

"I'll hold the boat while you unfasten him." Sawyer's angry gaze connected with hers.

Careful to hide her emotions as to not upset Maverick even more, she forced her voice to be soft. "Hold on tight. I'm going to get you out."

The water was waist-high, but the erratic movement made it difficult to manipulate. She dug her fingers into the side of the boat, pinching a good grip, and threw her boot up on the side. The boat swung away from her, causing her foot to fall back into the water. "Hold it still."

Sawyer moved to the other side and bent over the edge of the boat, pinning it under his arms. "Try it again."

She dug her fingers in again and swung her foot fast. Her boot caught long enough for her to pull herself inside. *Hurry. Hurry.* Her mind repeated the words as she fell to her knees beside her son and her hands worked to free him. The belt had a pinch clasp on it, and she quickly released it. She pulled Maverick into her arms in a hug.

"Let me get y'all to the bank. Stay seated—"

A gunshot blasted, instantly followed by two more shots, making her jump. While holding Maverick against her chest, she reached for her gun.

Sawyer stumbled in the water and then got back to his feet. "Hold on. Someone shot the rope."

"Were you hit?"

"No."

She clung to Maverick while searching the bank for the shooter. Behind her, a blur of red disappeared through the trees on the side they had just traveled. The boat moved swiftly down the river. Maverick clung to her neck, making it difficult to move.

Sawyer reached for the boat, but it moved from underneath his grasp and kept going.

"Come on." She held out her hand to him.

"Help him," Maverick begged.

Sawyer dove into the water and swam, but his effort made little difference. She put her hand in the river against the current trying to do anything to slow it down. He tried grasping it again, but his hand slipped from the rubber material.

"Try again," she yelled. She kept her hand fanned out in the water. Just a few more inches.

Sawyer was tiring as he moved with the current. This

time, he lunged for the boat and grasped it. She grabbed his arm and tugged to help him get inside. He took a deep breath, determination crossing his face, before he lurched, thrusting his body on the side of the boat and climbing in.

"Do you see any paddles or way to guide this thing?" she asked.

He looked around. "There's nothing. But…" He pointed.

She turned. A huge tree draped across the water and the craft was heading straight for it. She and Sawyer both stuck their arms out. Sawyer's hit the tree, and he shoved the boat away from it.

The noise of the river grew louder. Dread descended on her as she knew what she would see before she saw it. Falls were up ahead. "Sawyer!"

"I see it." He hurriedly moved to the front of the boat. "Hang on to Maverick."

There was no time to change the course of the boat. Sawyer wrapped his arms around the two of them and pulled them against his chest. He bowed his head. "God, help us."

Mallory closed her eyes and repeated the same words as Sawyer.

Water sprayed them, the boat bouncing roughly as it hit a rock on her side. And then they were falling.

Her stomach went into her throat, and her grasp on Maverick tightened as he screamed.

They plunged into the cold water. Sawyer's arm came down on her head. But Maverick was no longer in her grasp. She gasped for air as she tried to get her head above the surface. The current swirled around, and for a moment, she lost her bearings.

"Mav!" As her body continued to propel down the river, she looked for him. Her side slammed into a rock, and then she saw him flailing. The current was slower but there were more rocks. She dove for him, caught his hand and hauled him against her.

He gasped for air and gagged. When his lungs cleared, he let out a loud cry. "Get me out of here. I don't like it!"

"I've got you," she said. "I will protect you."

"I don't like it," he squealed again.

"Sawyer!" She looked around for him but didn't see him. All she saw was the inflatable boat disappearing downstream.

"I'm here."

She turned around and looked into his face as he swiped water from his eyes.

"We need to get to shore. Hang on to Maverick, and I'll get us there."

She wanted to argue, but her whole body was shaking from exhaustion. She didn't think she could swim another lick. Sawyer grabbed her bicep and tugged her toward the bank. As they drew closer, the current slowed and the river became shallow.

"Put your feet down," he said.

When she tried to stand, her foot slipped and she went down to her knee, but she managed to keep Maverick in her grasp. "Don't let go."

"I won't." Sawyer held out his other hand and took Maverick.

When she tried to stand again, her knees buckled, but Sawyer kept hold of her long enough for her to regain her balance. She'd often heard the expression of legs feeling like spaghetti, but this was much worse than anything else she'd felt before.

Sawyer followed behind her, carrying Maverick. When they got to the bank, both she and Sawyer collapsed on the ground. He held Maverick close. "Are you okay, lil' buddy?"

Mav frowned but nodded. "I'm cold. I don't want to get in the water no more."

He gave him a smile. "We'll get you warmed up as soon as we get to our truck."

"'Kay."

Sawyer removed his gun from his holster at his waist, and water poured from it. He proceeded to remove the clip only to see it, too, was dripping wet.

She did the same with both of her weapons. "We could take them apart and let them dry."

"Our ammunition is soaked."

Shooting bullets that had been submerged in water was dangerous. It's possible they might fire okay, or they could misfire or cause a squib load where the bullet lodges in the barrel. "This isn't good."

Sawyer looked around. "I don't see the kidnappers. I have more ammunition in the truck."

"Me, too. I doubt they could make it this far down river that quick." She also surveyed the area. "I don't see anyone else."

"Me, either. Thankfully, schools hadn't let out yet so it's a little early for most campers."

Maverick climbed out of Sawyer's lap and moved in front of her. "I don't want to get back in the water."

A laughed escaped her. "Me, neither." She ran her hand on his face. "Were you hurt?"

He shook his head no. "I didn't like them. I yelled for you, and the one in the basketball shirt told me to shut up." His lip puckered.

Sawyer said, "They shouldn't have done that. We'll make sure they get in trouble for that."

"Good."

Mallory asked, "What kind of basketball shirt?"

"It had a big ball on it. The shirt was blue."

"You were such a big boy, Mav. I'm proud of you." Poor guy had been a part of so much danger the last couple of days, she was afraid it would take him a while to heal from this. "Have you ever seen the man before? Was it the same one who tried to take you at the farm?"

He nodded and his eyebrows drew. "Yeah. I don't like him."

She hugged him. "Me, either."

"It's time we get moving. I figure the men have left, but they could check to see if their plan succeeded." Sawyer climbed to his feet and returned his weapons back into their holsters.

When she moved to stand, she let out a small grunt with the effort. She couldn't remember ever being this exhausted. She, too, put her weapons away and hoped she would feel more energized once they got to moving. "I'm thinking we walk up the hill and go from there."

"I agree. If the men try to find us, it'll be along the river." He grasped her arm, pulling her close. "Are you certain you're okay? You're not hurt?"

She stared up into his warm brown eyes that used to evoke a feeling of trustworthiness. Funny the feeling was still there. "I'm fine, but I'll be even better once we make it back to my truck."

He leaned in. For a moment, she thought he might kiss her as their gazes held. Then he turned away and held out his hands to Maverick. "Would you mind if I carry you? I'm sure there's poison ivy in the area, and I don't want you itching."

Maverick looked at her.

"Go ahead, honey. Sawyer is right. There are plants out here that feel like mosquito bites."

He wrinkled up his lip and then leaped into Sawyer's arms.

She was glad Sawyer had phrased it like it was the plants he was concerned about. No doubt, Mav would've preferred to walk and not be carried like a baby. It was a phrase he said often when Mallory tried to carry him. Sawyer's broad back showed through the wet shirt, making her take notice of his athletic build. No doubt work on the ranch and an active lifestyle had paid off. She reminded herself she was in Cedar Hollow to solve a cold case, not notice the scenery.

They headed uphill, the trek not as easy since there was no evident trail. They weaved around brush and briars.

"I'm hungry," Maverick complained.

It was getting late, and they'd eaten an early lunch, too. "We'll get something at the store on the way to the ranch."

He frowned but didn't say anything more.

Thirty minutes went by, maybe more. Her feet ached and her jeans were still damp. She hoped her boots didn't cause blisters. Normally, she packed extra socks and shoes just in case something like this arose, but the extra pack had been burned up in her Jeep. "Does it seem like we should've made it back to the road yet?"

Sawyer said, "Maybe. It makes me wonder if the road comes down this far or if it ends further south. We traveled a decent distance down the river."

"I hope you're wrong." She sighed. "I can't wait to get out of these wet clothes."

"Me, too. By the time we get back, they might be dry."

She hoped it didn't take that long.

"I'm hungry," Maverick said again. "When can we stop?"

"Hang in there, son." Sawyer patted him on the back. "This is a tough walk, but cowboys get used to working all day and then we get a great meal. What would you like to get when we stop?"

"Chicken nuggets and fries."

"That's some of my favorites," Sawyer agreed. "Okay. It's a deal. Maverick gets to pick the menu."

Mallory couldn't believe he just called Maverick his son, even though Mav didn't appear to notice. She glared at Sawyer until it got his attention.

"What?"

"Did you do that on purpose? Call him your..." She mouthed, "Son?"

His face slackened. "No. But it's past time. He needs to know, Mal. You tell him or I will. I'm not going to wait any longer."

She appreciated everything Sawyer had done for them, but once she told their son, there'd be no going back. For someone who hadn't been around kids much, the cowboy was patient and intuitive when it came to Maverick. Sadness tugged at her, thinking about what all he'd missed out on. Not just for Sawyer's sake, but also hers. It would've been nice to have him around when Maverick caught RSV and spent three days in hospital. Or when he was fifteen months old, and she hurt herself during training by spraining her ankle on a steep descent in the canyon. She'd spent a week on crutches. They'd lived on the second floor of an apartment. Getting Maverick up the stairs had been a challenge, not to mention carrying groceries.

"Well? What are you thinking?" Sawyer asked.

"Just thinking what a natural you are with kids." She sighed. "There were times you would've almost came in handy."

He stopped in a small clearing and looked at her. "If I'd known, I would've been there. You know that."

They started walking again. She said, "I thought you knew the whole time. Please, don't rub it in."

"I don't mean to, but I'm still having a hard time wrapping my mind around it. What I missed. What *he* missed."

She noticed he was careful not to spell out what they were talking about in front of Maverick. "Sorry for bringing it up. It's probably hard to believe, but it wasn't a picnic for me, either."

"I'm sure it wasn't. I don't like that, either." Sawyer's strides grew longer and more determined.

She recognized the action as him being frustrated. It was funny because it'd been five years since they'd dated, but he hadn't changed all that much. He was stubborn. Determined. Self-confident. But also, kind—in his own tough way.

"Sawyer, you're right." She turned to look at her son. "Maverick, Mama needs to tell you something."

"What?" He looked up at her.

Sawyer looked over his shoulder at her, waiting.

She'd put it off so long, she didn't know how to phrase it. Something moved in the brush, making her stop in her tracks. "What was that?"

He halted also. "I don't know." They both stood still for a few seconds before he motioned her forward. "Must be an animal."

The wind picked up as the sun began to set, making chill bumps appear on her arms. "Do you need me to carry Maverick? I'm sure your arm could use a break."

"I'm good. I want to get back to the truck before dark."

Darkness was an hour or two away, and she didn't think they'd have a problem with the timeline. Something moved again in the brush. This time she kept going, but she kept her eye on the brush from where the noise came from.

"I think I see the camp up ahead. We must've gone too far east, past the road we drove in on."

At first, she didn't see it, but then the tent's orange and gray shape came into view in the distance. "Finally."

She was so relieved to be almost back to the truck and looking forward to getting something to eat and out of the damp clothes, it took a minute for the sounds to register in her mind.

Sawyer stuck his hand out. "Pigs."

Her mind wrestled with what he was saying. Wild pigs. Suddenly, warnings from Deacon to never approach a wild pig went through her mind. She whispered, "Let's just move quietly around them."

Maverick looked in the direction of the pigs. "What's that, Mommy?"

She put her finger to her lips. "Shh." She motioned to Sawyer. "Let me have him."

Maverick came to her. She said, "You need to be really quiet. Those are pigs. We don't want to scare them."

Most of the time pigs would run, but occasionally, if you startled them or got between a sow and her piglet, the mom would attack. Even though it was rare, pigs had been known to kill people.

Mallory moved as quietly as possible. The sun would be going down soon, and she had no desire to be out here in the dark. Something scattered among the leaves, and her steps faltered. She swallowed hard and took off again, careful not to hit branches or thorns, shoving everything out of the way as she maneuvered down the faint trail.

The trail veered to the right and down into a narrow creek. As she tromped into it, movement again carried to her from the woods. Not stopping, she continued down the creek bed while looking up and trying to keep an eye out.

She was glad Sawyer was with her but wished their ammo wasn't soaked. Was it worth taking the chance of using the compromised bullets? No.

A shadow moved across the rocky bed, making her jerk to a stop. She looked into the trees but saw nothing except for the branches blowing in the wind. Was it the kidnappers or pigs?

Sawyer gently pushed her in the back. "Keep going. I'll follow you and keep a look out."

A faint trail led to the left, and it wasn't as steep as the other sides. Abruptly she took that route when her foot came down on a large pine cone, making her ankle twist. Pain shot up her leg, but she kept moving.

Darkness fell faster in the shadow of the trees. A silhouette presented itself under the shadow of a huge pecan tree.

"They're over here!"

The man's voice spurred Mallory into action. She made a beeline in the direction of her truck while carrying Maverick.

She swallowed hard. *Please, God, be with us.*

A small clearing emerged in front of her. Something moved on the other side, and her steps stuttered. She simply watched for a couple of seconds. It was pigs, like Sawyer had suggested. Instead of going around, they had walked right up on them.

She kept her voice down to avoid startling the wild animals and whispered to Maverick, "Remember to be real quiet." At his nod, Mallory stepped backward while keeping her eyes on the wild beasts. A couple of them watched her.

Their grunting and squealing had stopped. Another ten feet and the pigs went back to eating. Her heart raced uncontrollably as she put distance between them. She might make it without disturbing them or sending them into a frenzy. The smaller pigs on the edge of the herd squealed and ran among the older ones. Mallory swallowed hard, waiting.

A man with scraggly red hair and his arm in a sling yelled something in a high-pitched voice. "I don't see them!"

Another male voice gruffly replied, "Keep looking. We don't leave until we find them."

She couldn't worry about them right now. Suddenly the pigs became agitated, and carrying Maverick, Mallory knew she couldn't outrun them. Sawyer's strong grip clamped down on her shoulder. She turned, and he pointed. A pine tree that had blown over was leaning into a huge pecan tree.

"Get up there," he said. He grabbed a thick branch from the ground.

She scrambled up just as the pigs ran in her direction. Mallory's boots slipped as she attempted to climb the knobby trunk, making her lose her grip on Maverick. He slid back to the ground. Her heart exploded in her chest.

"Get back!" Sawyer swung the limb, hitting a female pig in the head.

She grasped Maverick's outstretched hands and tugged him up. His legs barely made it out of the way just in time to escape the sharp tusk of the angry sow.

"Over here." The voice of the man with the long hair carried in the woods.

The pigs circled one another, riling each other up. The sow turned her attention to Sawyer and charged.

"Sawyer!" Mallory tried to make room on the tree trunk, but she wasn't quick enough. Sawyer dashed for the nearest tree and wrapped his arms around it, shimming up it as fast as he could. The pig rammed the bottom of his leg before he lifted it above her head.

Maverick cried and fastened his arms around her neck. “I want to go home!”

“You’re safe with me. Sawyer and I will protect you.” As she whispered the words of comfort, she wondered if they would make it out alive. A herd of wild pigs and two kidnappers wanted to kill them.

And their ammunition was worthless.

Sawyer’s leg was on fire, but he thought it was more from the impact. As far as he could tell, it wasn’t bleeding. The pigs continued to grunt a few feet under the trunk that Mallory stood on. She braced herself for balance and hugged it with all of her might, obviously realizing her life depended on it. Losing her grip could prove fatal.

Mallory had always been a competent officer. The first time he’d noticed her was when they were taking law enforcement classes at the community college. During the second week of classes, the instructor offered a demonstration and asked for volunteers. Five students were put in front of the class to role-play arresting a suspect. During the exercise, Mallory shot her laser gun at a man, disabling him. Sawyer had been confused why she reacted by shooting until he realized the man had been an armed second suspect he hadn’t noticed. After that day, he began to take notice of everything she did. During their first training with a simulator, she’d been the only student in the class to successfully deescalate a situation and apprehend a suspect. Without incident.

His attraction grew from there until a few weeks later when he got up the nerve to ask her out on a date. She declined the first two times, but the third time was the charm. The relationship grew from there.

Running feet on the forest floor had him turning to look over his shoulder. A man with red hair wearing a blue T-shirt with a basketball on it ran into the clearing with a gun in his hand. His other arm was in a sling.

Mallory hollered, “Watch out!”

The pigs snorted and ran the guy’s way. The piglets squealed and formed a moving circle as the huge sow charged the man. Her tusk hit him above the knee, sending him flying back onto the ground, his gun flying into the brush. The man yelled an obscenity as he tried to get back to his feet, but another adult pig hit him. The man screamed.

Sawyer had seen lots of violent things, but even he squeezed his eyes shut, not wanting to watch, and kept his grip on the pine tree’s trunk. He looked up as the man struggled to his feet, fell to his knee one more time before he was rammed again.

A glance at Mallory showed Maverick had buried his face in his mama’s chest.

More writhing on the forest floor and then all fell eerily silent except for the grunting of the pigs.

Sawyer wanted to climb down the tree and get them to safety, but he needed to make certain the pigs would not attack again.

“Chad?” The kidnapper with the gruff voice came running up the hill through the woods straight for them. “Where are you?”

Sawyer kept an eye on the pigs as the smaller ones disappeared into the trees and the three larger ones remained where the man went down.

A man entered the clearing on the other side with a gun in his hand. It was difficult to tell in the darkness, but the man looked to be in his thirties. Sawyer tried to see if the man wore a ring on his pinkie finger. Something reflected, but it might have been the gun. "Chad?" the guy kept his voice down like he knew something was going on. "Where are you?"

The same big sow who'd charged Chad snorted as she trotted toward the man.

Sawyer jumped from the tree and hurried to Mallory. "Let's go." He took Maverick from her, and they ran for the truck.

Several shots blasted, but the bullets didn't land anywhere near them. The shooter must've been aiming at the pigs. As they ran past the camping site, the man shouted something. Two more shots went off.

Maverick didn't say a word as he put him in the back seat. Mallory jumped in on the driver's side and started the engine. As she backed up to turn around, he leaned over the seat and buckled Maverick in his booster seat.

Before she drove out of the camping area, he said. "Pull up to the GMC and the Kawasaki."

He jotted down the license plates numbers.

The man ran out of the trees aiming the gun at them.

"Watch out." The bullet hit the side of his door, and Mallory hit the accelerator. "Lean over in the seat, Mav. Keep your head low."

Sawyer leaned down and hurried to find his other box of ammunition in his backpack. He found it and loaded his gun. The shooting stopped. He turned around to Maverick. "Are you okay, lil' buddy?"

His face wrinkled up in a frown. "Yeah. I wanna go home."

He patted him on the leg. "We're headed back to the ranch. We'll get something to eat first."

"Okay." His whiny tone told Sawyer he wasn't too happy.

"Mama is getting us out of here. Hang on and we'll get something to eat like Sawyer said." She glanced at him. "Can you reload mine, too?"

"Yeah." Using a towel, he wiped down his gun to make certain it was dry before loading it with fresh bullets. Then he did the same with her guns.

She pulled onto the dirt road they had come down and glanced at him. "I'd like to go back and arrest that guy, but I don't want to do anything to endanger anyone."

Sawyer caught her meaning without her having to say their son's name. "You need backup. From now on, we don't go anywhere without at least one, preferably two, of my brothers with us."

"I so agree."

He checked his cell phone, but it was wet, not that he believed there was a signal anyway. "You don't happen to have an extra cell phone, do you?"

"I did, but it was in my Jeep."

"I was afraid of that." He handed Mallory her weapon and stored his away. "I'm going to use the towel to dry my cell phone. Let me have yours and I'll do the same."

She shook her head. "I doubt it works, but it doesn't hurt to try." She fished her phone from her pocket and handed it to him.

"The guy with the basketball T-shirt had a bandaged arm. I assume that was the man who drove the Kawasaki that we saw last night."

"I agree with you." Her eyes cut to him. "You believe that whole thing—the kidnapping, the tent and camper gear, and the boat was all a setup to get us up here and make it look like we'd had an accident?"

"I do. Whoever killed three people thought they could

get away with three more." The thought at how close the plan came to working tasted sour in his mouth.

By the time they made it to the closest convenience store—a hole-in-the-wall place that sold "gas, worms and unique gifts"—he'd completed his task of drying and restarting their phones. Both came on, but the screen on his flashed. "You want to see if yours works?"

Sitting in the parking lot, she took it from him. "It's showing two bars. That surprises me."

She hit Hawk's number. When he answered, she put it on speaker. "This is Mallory. You're on speaker, and Sawyer is here."

"Have you gotten Maverick back?"

"Affirmative. The brave guy is with us right now." Sawyer glanced over his shoulder and gave him an assured nod. Maverick stared at him, but Sawyer knew he was absorbing the compliment.

"What's your location?"

"We're at Jammer's Jambalaya on Farm to Market Road 29." Farm to Market Roads in Texas were rural highways that mostly didn't have shoulders. "There were two suspects. One named Chad, and no name yet on the other. Chad had a confrontation with swine and may not make it." Sawyer was careful not to be too detailed as he didn't want Maverick to understand. "The other one is still healthy. I'll text you the license plate numbers of both the truck and the motorcycle."

"I'm close. ETA is two minutes."

"Okay. See you in a few." After he disconnected, he said, "I'm tempted to go back to the campsite to see if our man is still there, but I don't want to leave you two alone here."

She shook her head. "I'm the Texas Ranger on the case. If anyone returns, it should be me."

He frowned. "I don't like that any better."

"Me, either." She looked in the rearview mirror at Maverick. "We can't let our guard down. Where's Cash and Emma?"

If Mallory was suggesting Emma help protect them, she was more concerned than she admitted out loud. Not that he didn't feel the same way. He didn't care what measures they had to take, he wasn't about to let their son wind up in the hands of the kidnappers again. Or Mallory.

Hawk's big black truck pulled into the lot. It was time to make a decision, and no matter what they chose, Sawyer felt like they were surrounded by danger.

TWELVE

After Hawk left the convenience store, Sawyer said to her, "It's time to tell him."

Mallory didn't have to ask what he was referring to. She turned around in the seat and decided to get it over with. Rip the Band-Aid off. "Maverick, I need to tell you something."

"What?"

"Come here." She leaned over the seat and unbuckled him and waited for him to stand on the floorboard. She wrapped her arm around his waist over the console. "You like Sawer, right?"

Mav nodded. "Yeah. He's a cowboy."

She couldn't help but smile. Her throat suddenly became dry, and she swallowed. She admonished herself again, *Rip the Band-Aid off.* "Sawyer is your daddy."

Sawyer glanced over his shoulder at them.

Their son blinked and looked in awe. "He is? My daddy's a cowboy?"

Her smile broadened. "He sure is. Are you okay with that?"

"Yeah!" He threw his arms above his head.

"I'm…" Sawyer cleared his throat. "I'm glad, too, son."

He turned and wrapped Maverick in a hug while she still held him.

After Maverick was buckled back up, he stared at the back of Sawyer's head but didn't say anything.

Mallory didn't know what she was expecting, but she had thought Mav would have many questions. Now that she thought about it, that was probably silly of her. It might take time for him to truly understand how this might change his life.

"Thank you."

The whisper had her glancing over at Sawyer. She found him staring at her, his warm eyes dancing with emotion.

"You're welcome. Would it be okay if we waited to tell your family until after this is over? It's their right to know, but I just feel like everything is coming at me at once." She rubbed her temples.

Sawyer kept his voice low. "I'd rather not instruct my boy to keep it a secret."

"That's a fair request. If he tells—" she shrugged "—he tells."

"Agreed."

Twenty minutes after Hawk left to check out the campsite, he pulled back into the parking lot. Mallory could only guess he didn't have big news, or he wouldn't have returned so quickly. All three of them had agreed it would be best for Sawyer and her to stay with Maverick while Hawk went to see if the kidnappers were still there.

She rolled down her window.

Hawk rolled down his passenger side window. "The tent is still there and the motorcycle, but the truck is gone. I found where it looked like the body had been, but it was gone."

"He's gone?" She looked at Sawyer. "I wonder if he was afraid that the basketball guy would be identified."

"Sounds like it." Sawyer slapped his leg. "I hate that the guy got away. The truck hasn't gone by here, so he must've known another exit."

"I did find one thing." Hawk held up a gun using a screwdriver so he wouldn't leave prints. "It's a Smith and Wesson SD 40."

"Really? That's the same kind that went missing from the evidence room. Hopefully, if it's proven to be the same one, it will help us figure out why someone took it or it might also give us a name." Mallory added, "I reported the incident to the local sheriff's department since it's out of Eagle County's jurisdiction. I also talked with Sheriff Copeland. As soon as Wyndam County deputies are out here, we need to get something to eat and go back to the ranch. Copeland was nice enough to send a deputy for extra protection to the ranch, so we can put Maverick to bed."

Hawk put a finger in the air as if to tell them he had one more thing to add. "I meant to tell you, I went by Bo's, Wilson's brother, earlier. He seemed to be forthcoming and didn't come off angry like his parents, but he had no new information. I'll dig deeper if you want me to, but my gut says he's not involved."

"That's okay." Mallory's gaze fixed on his brother. "I trust your instinct."

"I don't want to go to bed," Maverick whined. "I'm hungry."

Both Sawyer and she glanced at the back seat.

Sawyer said, "Me, too." The words were no more out of his mouth than a Wyndam County deputy's cruiser pulled into the parking lot. "Hang on, buddy. Just a few more minutes."

He looked back at Mallory. "Let's finish talking after we visit with the deputies and are back at the ranch."

Fifteen minutes later, they had made their report to the officers, and Hawk gave them the gun he'd found. Before he climbed into the truck, Sawyer called, "You coming with us, Hawk?"

The oldest Cantrell brother nodded. "I'm going to follow you."

She said, "Good. Let's go. I could use something to eat, too."

They left the parking lot, and Hawk pulled out behind them. Sawyer agreed that with one of kidnappers out of commission, there probably wasn't a great chance they'd be attacked tonight, but they weren't willing to take a chance. They picked up burgers at a drive-through, and all of them ate in silence. Poor Maverick fell asleep with two fries still in his grasp. He had to be dog-tired.

Cash, Emma and Nora were all waiting for them when they got back to the ranch. Thankfully, the drive home had been uneventful. After she dressed and put Maverick to bed, Sawyer came into the room and kissed him on the head.

She whispered, "Someone might see you."

"I don't care. Do you realize if the worst would've happened tonight…? If he wouldn't have made it back, our son would've never known I'm his daddy. I don't want to be a part-time dad."

Someone walked down the hall, and Mallory noticed their steps faltered before continuing down the stairs. Sawyer took a deep breath as he continued to stare at their son as if he didn't care that a family member might have overheard him. "Not now. We'll figure out the visitation details later. There's too much going on."

"I've waited long enough. I don't want to go against you, Mal, but you're not being fair. It might be impossible, but I've already grown attached to him."

She stared up at the ceiling. It wasn't impossible at all. He was right. They needed to make a plan that would work for all three of them. She'd had sole custody for so long, she knew it would be hard to share the reins. She rubbed her hand gently across the top of Maverick's head. But he deserved the best.

"Deputy Woods is here," Hawk yelled from downstairs.

She hurried to the kitchen so she could give her statement. Wyndam County deputies did not find the kidnapper's body, either, but planned to investigate the scene more in the morning.

It was well past midnight before she made it upstairs and got ready for bed. As tired as she was after she climbed under the covers, sleep wouldn't come. Visions of Maverick being tied inside the boat in the river kept replaying through her mind. Sawyer was right. If Maverick hadn't survived—a thought that was too painful to consider—he wouldn't know Sawyer was his daddy. Giving up was not something she ever considered. Ever. Not when a drunk driver had pulled a knife on her when she was a state trooper. Not when her fellow Texas Ranger had been threatened by a group of thugs, and Mallory had stepped in the line of fire to defend him, and they had wound up apprehending two of the thugs that night, and the other three were arrested the following week.

But her son had never been this close to being hurt before.

As much as being a Texas Ranger was a part of her identity, so was being a mom. She wasn't certain how to combine the two. Even as the thought came to her, she knew it wasn't true. Being a mom was the most important thing in her life. She said her prayers, asking for protection and being grateful for Sawyer and the rest of his family.

The next morning, she awoke early. Maverick was still sound asleep, so she was careful not to wake him. Guilt weighed on her for all that she had put him through. Deep down, she knew it was the actions of the killers who'd caused the problem, but she couldn't help but remind herself that investigating this case had been her decision.

Doubt niggled at her conscience. Maybe Sawyer and Kari had been right all along. Sam was dead and no amount of evidence would bring him back to life.

As she went into the bathroom to get dressed, she shook her head. No. She was in law enforcement. She was meant to solve crimes, and that presented a certain number of risks. Maverick could and would be kept safe.

When she went down for breakfast, she found Shaylee and Cash in the kitchen.

Mallory greeted them with a "Good morning."

Shaylee reciprocated the gesture and Cash simplified his reply to "Mornin'."

"There's leftover eggs, bacon and biscuits. Help yourself." The cook pointed to the covered dishes on the stove.

"Thanks." Even after her burger meal last night, Mallory was hungry. She helped herself to a plate and sat on a stool at the bar. "Is Sawyer up, yet?"

"I've been up a couple of hours." Sawyer strode into the kitchen dressed in normal attire of boots, jeans and his denim Western shirt with the sleeves rolled up. His hair was combed back. Since he normally had a five-o'clock shadow, it was impossible to tell if he had shaved.

"What have you been working on? I need to get a plan

for the day, and then I'll call my lieutenant to give him an update."

"Hawk is running the license plates of the truck and motorcycle. If he hasn't already learned the owners' identities, he should soon."

"Good." Mallory poured herself a glass of milk before sitting at the bar. "I still feel like we're missing something obvious. I need to call Rosemary, one of Tilda's coworkers. Someone has to remember something."

Cash said, "I'm available today for security. My job is to stay with y'all whether you stay here or go somewhere."

"That eases my mind." She looked at Sawyer. "Have you said a blessing for the food?"

"Uh, not yet." He glanced around the room before he bowed his head and said grace.

She hoped she hadn't put him on the spot, but she felt that was better than bowing her head and saying a silent prayer while they all looked on. She remembered Deacon and Nora before every meal said grace, so she assumed the family still did.

After a few silent moments, Cash said, "I wish Clive were here, too, just to add to the numbers."

She hadn't seen Clive since she'd returned. "There's no need. I trust you all for protection. You said he'd just gotten married and had a baby girl."

Sawyer grabbed a piece of bacon from the dish. "Yeah. He seems happy."

"I can't wait to meet his wife. Tasting the food she makes, I already love her, but I hope they're not here until the murderers are behind bars." When Mallory pushed to reopen the Pennington and Newport files, she didn't anticipate so many people could be in harm's way. If the killer and/or killers came to the ranch, everyone could be in danger. "What about your mom?"

"She's out for her morning run." Sawyer shook his head like he didn't understand why she did it. "She took Mollie Beth with her."

Cash chuckled. "Don't look so down, Mallory. We're in security. We're trained for this."

Mallory forced a smile. "I realize that. And you're all good at your job."

"I'm hungry."

She looked up to see Maverick standing in the doorway, his hair sticking up on the side of his head. "Good morning."

He glanced around at everyone and then ran to her, burying his face in her lap like he didn't like being the center of attention.

"Would you like something to eat?" she asked.

Shaylee added, "We have cereal or bacon and eggs. Or if there's something else you'd like."

He looked up and stood up. "Do you have doughnuts?"

"Hmm. No." Shaylee's eyebrows went up. "I have biscuits, though, and I can make chocolate gravy."

"Chocolate gray-bee?"

Mallory laughed. "It's gravy, and it's good. You'd love it." She turned her attention to the cook. "There's no need to go to all that trouble."

"It's no trouble. The biscuits are already made. The gravy won't take two minutes."

Before Mallory could argue, Shaylee had already got out the saucepan. She remembered the first time she'd eaten chocolate gravy over biscuits. It had been a Sunday morning before church, and Nora had made it for the family. Mallory had been skeptical, but she fell in love with it.

Deacon and the whole family would sit down at the table and eat together. Mallory had found that terribly inviting.

Twenty minutes later, Maverick had eaten three biscuits, and sticky brown goo stuck to his upper lip.

"Come on. Let's go upstairs and get you cleaned up." Little about the case had been discussed except about trying to learn the identity of the kidnappers. It was tempting to relax today and not think about the case, but she knew that was impossible. The danger would only grow worse, and giving the killers time to regroup could only benefit them. They needed to move and move quickly.

"Mallory." Sawyer stood outside the bedroom door. "Hawk matched the license plate with the owners. I'm sorry to say, both plates were stolen less than forty-eight hours ago."

Her shoulders fell, and she addressed Maverick. "Put your clean clothes on." She closed the bedroom door and stepped into the hallway with Sawyer. "They are starting to get more organized. That's not good."

"Exactly. I doubt the kidnappers were the ones who committed the murders. I get the feeling they were hired, and the person behind it has money and power."

"I get the same feeling." The weight on her shoulders grew heavier. "The only way to stop the attacks is to learn who is behind the murders. We need to move fast…"

"And carefully…" he added.

His words seemed to sum up the situation perfectly.

Sawyer hadn't slept at all. He didn't like the feeling of being pinned down. The kidnappers had successfully made him second-guess leaving the house, and that aggravated him. On top of the danger, he wanted to be able to acknowledge Maverick as his boy to his family. To everyone…, Later that morning, he walked to the office in the barn and found Hawk working away on his laptop. “Have you found anything more?”

His brother swiveled his chair around to face him. “Here you go.” He held out two cheap cell phones to him. “This should tide you two over until you’re able to either get your other ones repaired or replaced.”

“Thanks.”

“To answer your question, I haven’t found anything more yet. I went over the files Mallory shared with me. Maybe we should visit the Pennington’s neighbor Harold Shultz again. The one who saw the car parked outside that night.”

“I was planning to do that already until my plans were hijacked yesterday.”

Sawyer turned to see Mallory enter the office with Maverick at her heels.

Maverick asked, “Can I see the horses?”

Sawyer smiled at seeing his son standing there.

Emma hollered from the barn’s large double doors. “I was just about to ask if Maverick wanted to help me with Parker.”

Sawyer smiled. “That sounds like a great idea. Can you stay in the barn?”

“Sure. This is the perfect place.”

Hawk was staring at Sawyer when he turned back to him, a question in his expression.

Mallory seemed to notice and joined in. “We need to find the owner of that car. And if it’s a sports car, hopefully it will not be as difficult to locate as a pickup.”

“True.” The number of trucks far outweighed the number of sports cars.

Hawk said, “Why don’t you let me go see the neighbor, uh—” he glanced at the paper in his hand “—Harold

Shultz. That way the three of you can stay here. Cash and Emma will be here."

Sawyer looked at Mallory. "It's your investigation, but I agree it would be better for us to stick together at the ranch."

"Okay." She put her hands in the air. "I don't like it, but it would be the safest choice. Let me call Mr. Shultz and set up the meeting."

"Here's a burner phone if yours is not working."

"I appreciate it, but mine is still working so far." After Mallory stepped out of the office to make the call, Hawk said, "You're getting awful close to the boy. Do you think that's a good idea?"

Sawyer wanted to tell him the truth that Maverick was his son, but Mal didn't want to tell his family yet. He disagreed with her on waiting to tell his family, but with everything going on, he didn't want to put pressure on her. "The boy was abducted and has seen more dangerous acts than any four-year-old should have to witness. I know what I'm doing."

Hawk squinted at him like he was trying to get a read on him. The conversation needed to be reverted back to the original topic. "Someone with money is behind this."

"Are you thinking drugs? None of the victims had ever been in trouble for using or selling."

He shook his head. "Not necessarily, but perhaps. I keep going back to Wilson Newport. I knew both Phillip and Tilda well. I can't see them being involved in anything dangerous, which leaves Wilson. His family is angry and is not quite as upstanding as the Penningtons."

Hawk leaned back in his chair. "Yet, Wilson was at Phillip and Tilda's house. Why was he there if they had nothing in common?"

Sawyer stared his older brother in the eyes. "I don't

know. The police believed Sam murdered the three because he broke into the house to steal and was caught in the act, panicked and killed them. Even they didn't build the case against Sam because they believed he had a disagreement with them."

Mallory returned to the office. "Then we need to look closer at the three victims. Even though Tilda's parents and coworkers had stated Tilda hadn't been dating anyone, at least two people claimed she'd been seeing someone. Also, Wilson supposedly hadn't been dating anyone. I want to double-check that. I'm hoping Rosemary can help me with that."

"I thought the only one who'd been seeing someone was Phillip, but nothing serious." Hawk came to his feet. "Cash can dig deeper on the internet to see if there's someone we missed."

"I've already done that about ten times." Mallory's eyebrows came together. "But maybe I missed something because I was too laser focused on certain things that I missed others. Someone else looking at it certainly can't hurt."

"It can happen." Sawyer knew she fought hard to let them help investigate. She'd been going over the facts of the case for years. More so, mentally she'd never taken a break from it. He knew what that could do to a person. Just like he'd gone over their failed relationship many times, even though he'd tried hard not to.

Mallory said, "Oh, and Harold said you can drop by anytime this morning. He's meeting someone for lunch at eleven-thirty, so any time before then."

Hawk climbed to his feet. "No better time like the present. Everything should be secure here."

"Let us know as soon as you know something. And be

careful." He knew the last part was unnecessary, but he found himself voicing it out loud anyway.

"You know it." Hawk grabbed his weapon from the desk and shoved it into the waist of his jeans before walking out of the office.

Sawyer scratched his forehead. "I'm going to sit down and go over the files again."

"I'll join you after I check on Maverick." She walked out of the office, and he followed her. Emma and Maverick stood at the far end of barn. Emma held a small clicker used in dog training as Maverick looked on in anticipation.

Emma said, "Stay," as she held out her hand in a halting motion.

Parker watched her intently, but he turned his head to look at Mallory. He jumped to his feet and jogged her way with his tail wagging.

Shaking her head, Emma hurried over. Parker looked at her and then sat, waiting for his treat.

"Nope. You must stay at least five seconds."

"I'm sorry. I didn't mean to distract him." Mallory rubbed him gently on the head.

"It's okay," Emma quickly said. "It's good I introduce him to distractions. He's learning, and we'll keep working on it."

Sawyer asked, "You sure you're okay with Maverick being with you?"

"Of course. He's a great helper." Emma smiled.

"I want a dog." With glistening eyes, Maverick looked up at Mallory.

She sighed. "We can talk about that later."

The way she said it made Sawyer believe they had already had this talk and that the answer had been no. When they went back into the office, he said, "I can help buy a dog if you want me to."

She chewed on her lip, a sure indication she was trying to control her response. "I don't need help paying for a dog. I work all day and barely have time to keep up with the house, doctor appointments, and especially all the other things I'd like to do with Maverick. The lack of money or desire is not the problem." Her words came faster. "I'm sure he'd love it if I could spend all day with him playing with animals."

"Whoa." He held his hands in the air. "I didn't mean anything by that. You know I would've been there for him and you if I had known he existed."

"I thought you knew." Her words were clipped. "I tried to tell you. It's not my fault you damaged your phone and waited to get it repaired. I still don't understand why you didn't get my letter."

"What letter?"

"Not only did I send a few texts, but also a letter. I sent it to the department."

"Mallory, I'm not blaming—"

She didn't slow down. "We come here and it's nonstop fun. Horses and dogs. Everyone seems to be in and out all day. Even Evie, his babysitter can't come close to competing, and neither can I."

"Mallory—"

"I am not normally with him like I have been during the last few days even. Don't you think I'd like to spend more time…"

He stepped forward and planted his lips on hers, halting her speech for a mere second.

She pulled away. "It's so frustrating…"

Placing his hand on the back of her neck, he pressed his

mouth to hers again. She didn't move away but actually kissed him back. The move brought memories flooding back like they had never been apart. Except it was even better than he remembered.

"Mama, come look." Maverick ran into the room unaware of what had just happened.

Mallory gently rubbed her hand across her lips. Her gaze connected with his and held for a moment before she turned. "Yes, honey, what is it?"

Sawyer whispered, "I'm not sorry about that so don't ask me to apologize."

She shook her head and hurried out of the door. He wasn't sure what to make of her reaction. He dropped into the leather chair and blankly stared at the laptop. There was no need for an apology, because he had no regrets whatsoever. He could still taste the tropical flavor of her gum, and it reminded him of times of the past. Mallory had a certain way about her that he'd always been attracted to. Not only her good looks and cute figure, but the way she talked fast when agitated. Maybe his timing hadn't been the smartest. They had a case to solve. A very dangerous case that could cost them their lives. *Way to go, Cantrell,* he inwardly chided himself.

Mallory had walked out of his life five years ago, and if he expected to work out a practical plan to spend time with Maverick, he'd just complicated the situation.

THIRTEEN

Mallory returned to Sawyer's bedroom and attempted to work on her laptop after calling Roy's Auto to tell them about the truck being in an accident. The manager wasn't happy, but he agreed to send out a wrecker to pick up the vehicle. Maverick was asleep, taking a nap even though it was unusual for him when he wasn't with Evie. She watched him as he breathed softly, curled up under a light blanket with horses on it.

Sawyer's kiss.

She couldn't get it out of her mind. She'd been emotional and Sawyer had done what he had years ago when she was going to leave him—disarm her with affection.

She wanted to be mad, and part of her was—she already decided she wasn't interested in a romance. Excitement also filled her, which aggravated her even more. Why? She would never consider renewing a relationship with him after he'd refused to stand beside her. Yes, he had tried to help her *face the truth* in his own way, but she'd needed a friend. A best friend. When the world turned its back on her, she desperately needed someone to stand beside her.

Tears built in her eyes, and she swiped them away. After all these years, it still hurt to know that he'd sided with everyone else. Even if he believed Sam was guilty, would it have hurt him to see the investigation through? Tell her he'd assist her until she was satisfied either way with the results? Maybe she had built up his love too big in her mind. Unobtainable expectations.

She didn't think so.

Still, she had Maverick to consider. Their boy was the forever link between them. Even if she or Sawyer married someone else, they would need to have a cordial relationship and not place Maverick in the crossfire. That included holidays. Summer vacations. And later, when Maverick graduated and got married. Sawyer and she would always be connected.

The thought depressed her, but also it kind of gave her a sense of peace to know someone would consistently be there. What was wrong with her? Why was she okay with Sawyer being a part of her life? The only conclusion she could come to was, besides her father who lived halfway across the country, she had no one else besides coworkers. Most of the Rangers were good people, but most had spouses or were in committed relationships. The really scary part was that even though Sawyer hadn't responded to the news of having a son, she had still felt connected to him every time she looked into Maverick's brown eyes, or when her son cocked his head at her and the adorable cleft in his chin lit up when he smiled.

She took a deep breath and looked up at the ceiling. Everything had changed now that Sawyer knew the truth and wanted to be a part of their son's life. Maybe they could start putting the past behind them for Maverick's sake. And for their sakes, too.

Hawk, Cash and Mallory gathered around the dining table while Sawyer looked in on Maverick in the living room. His son sat on the floor watching cartoons sandwiched between Mollie Beth and Parker. Sawyer couldn't help but think about how Maverick had quickly become a part of the family, including the animals and ranch lifestyle. His chest squeezed at the thought of him leaving in a few days for Amarillo. The drive was over six hours. Even if he and Mallory could work out a good visitation arrangement, it wouldn't be enough. How could he be a part-time dad?

When he strode into the dining room, he caught Mallory watching him. It was almost like she could read his thoughts. She, too, had melted into the Thunder Ridge Ranch scene, but he got the feeling she would deny it and turn tail and run as soon as this case was closed. Still, he wanted to see not only closure for her, but also justice for the three victims.

In true fashion, Hawk had little patience for sitting still and started the conversation before Sawyer took his seat. "Dr. Bourg claiming that he drove a BMW at the time of Tilda's death checked out. We're still digging into the claim Tilda was caught embezzling. We talked to Rosemary, the nurse, who no longer works for the doctor but moved to another practice. Rosemary confirmed there were several tense discussions behind closed doors before Tilda's death, and once she did overhear the words *stealing* and *fraud* being discussed in loud voices. According to the nurse, it was the doctor who'd used those terms."

Sawyer said, "So Tilda might have been caught stealing. I have a hard time believing that. I knew Phillip better than his sister, but that doesn't mean it didn't happen." He continued to pull up memories of Phillip. The family was good and honest. Hard workers. What he remembered of Tilda was she was the kid sister that was busy with a lot of school activities, from sports to making the honor roll.

"I found it a coincidence this was only days before her murder." Mallory folded her arms over her chest, a look he'd seen before. "Did you ask her if Tilda had a boyfriend?"

"Sorry. I didn't." Frustration crossed his angular jaw. "I can go see her again."

She grabbed a piece of cookie off of the plate in the center of the table. "That's okay. I'll give her a follow-up call. Were you able to get in touch with the doctor's son Cullum?"

Hawk shook his head. "Not yet. I've left two voicemails on his phone, but he has yet to call me back."

"I stopped by the clinic at the doctor's office, but Cullum wasn't in," Cash added. "I'll keep trying."

"I'm assuming there's been no visits to auto repair shops on thc kidnapper's truck," Mallory said.

"I'm afraid not," Cash said. "Not that that surprises me, though."

"Yeah, the only vehicle in the shop is my rented truck." Mallory tapped her fingers on the table before helping herself to the rest of the cookie she'd picked at. "Any progress on any of Wilson Newport's family?"

Everyone shook their head no at the samc time.

Sawyer said, "What about Wilson's friends, Lucas Hall and Bryce Brewer? I thought they were kind of troublemakers?"

"I did a shallow look at both Lucas and Bryce. Lucas's record is clean. Bryce had a couple of possessions of marijuana. He didn't do jail time for either offense."

"I agree neither sound like they could pull something like kidnapping or framing someone for murdering three people." It was frustrating that they were no closer to learning who would've committed the murders. "I think we should zoom out on Wilson's circle of friends. We're missing something."

When he glanced at Mallory, she stared at him for a moment before tapping her fingers on the table again. She said, "I agree. Did anyone know Wilson very well? He was a couple of years older than me, and I barely remember seeing him around town."

Cash said, "He was in my class, but we hung around different people. He wasn't in sports or FFA—Future Farmers of America. He was at the bottom of the class, grade wise."

"He had an older brother."

Everyone turned to see his mom in the kitchen. She sipped from a water bottle. "Neil was about twelve years older than Wilson. The only reason I remember him was Mrs. Newport was expecting Wilson at the same time as I was Cash. She'd made mention how it was like having two only children. My guess is that's why they had Bo a couple of years later."

Sawyer had no idea. It wasn't the first time discussing a case that if they'd just ask his mom, they would learn a thing or two.

Hawk strode into the room. "I've got some news."

Everyone looked his way.

"Dr. Bourg drove a white four-door BMW like he claimed, but did y'all know Cullum drove a blue metallic Jaguar?"

"No," he and Mallory said in unison. This could be the break they'd been looking for.

Hope filled Mallory. "I wonder if this is the car that Harold Shultz saw at the Pennington house the night of the murders."

"Definitely a possibility," Sawyer replied.

Mallory said, "I need to make a call to my lieutenant. I don't know if a judge will grant a search warrant for the car plus Cullum and Dr. Bourg's residences and offices, but it doesn't hurt to try. This could be our first big break."

"Make certain you have all your ducks in a row. We need this."

There was no need for Sawyer to remind her what they needed. She was very aware of how important it was to be patient and get all of her facts together. Her mind whirled with the information. Deep down, she doubted this would be enough for a judge to issue a warrant. She didn't even know what she hoped to find in Cullum and Dr. Bourg's residence or offices. "I need more."

Sawyer looked at her. "You need to build a solid case, but I see what you mean."

"Can we all work on getting a deep dive into Cullum's background? We need to do our homework."

"I'll get Hawk and Cash on it."

"I'll pull a background check." Her mind whirled at everything that needed to be done. "Can you or one of your brothers look to see if Cullum happened to receive a ticket or anything that would place him near the Pennington home close to the time of the murders? Also, make certain the opposite doesn't exist, like his car was parked in his own driveway at the time of the murders."

"I got it."

After he left the room, Mallory called her lieutenant with the possible find. Just as she was afraid of, his first words were, "You need more if you want a judge to issue a search warrant."

"Yes, sir. We're doing our homework right now. I just wanted to keep you informed of the progress."

"Foster, you're doing a good job, but you could benefit

from having another Texas Ranger on your team. There's been too many attacks for just one Ranger. I'm sending Barnett to assist you."

Dread filled her. It's not that she had anything against Ranger Sean Barnett, but she felt like catching him up on the case would slow down her momentum. She had only been with the department for a little over a year and knew she shouldn't argue. "Yes, sir. I appreciate it."

She clicked off and then called Rosemary. The older lady was at work and admitted she didn't have long to talk. Mallory asked her if Tilda had a boyfriend. The woman quickly said she remembered her talking about a man called Andy or Randy—she couldn't remember. After she hung up with Rosemary, she went to her room where she could concentrate. The laptop she'd borrowed from Emma was already on the bed, and she sat down and logged in on her work database, ready to find something that would provide justifiable reasons for a search warrant. The name Randy kept going through her mind, making it difficult to concentrate. Janet Jacobson's son was named Randy, and Kari had acted suspicious at the mention of the name. Janet's email was the reason she was granted permission to reopen this case.

She called Hawk on the phone and explained to him what she'd learned. He agreed to see what information he could find. Feeling better, she got back to work on Cullum.

Twenty minutes later, she had found Cullum had been charged with theft two times. Once while in college, he'd been accused of charging his roommate's credit card fourteen times for a total of just under eight thousand dollars over a period of two years. That was enough to be a felony in Texas, but the case was settled out of court. The second charge was for theft of four rims from a local tire shop. The value was over five thousand dollars. The owner didn't drop the charges, but the case was never brought before a judge.

Did the good doctor bail his son out of trouble?

The plaintiff in the wheel theft was Tire Castle, a family business off of Hwy 39, between Cedar Hollow and Meadowlark. She wrote down his information in her notes in case she needed to visit the owner.

A knock sounded on the door, and before Sawyer could make it all the way into the room, he asked, "Did you know Cullum was treated for a possible gunshot wound the day after the murders?"

"What? No." This could be a major break, and she didn't even try to keep the excitement out of her voice. "Where did he receive treatment? At his dad's clinic?"

"Yeah. Cash was talking with a radiology technician, Bowen Moore, at the hospital. It was someone he'd talked to a year ago on a case of theft in the doctor/employee lounge. Several items, including iPads, wallets and personal items, went missing. Bowen had been one of the victims who had his Rolex watch he'd inherited from his dad stolen. Even though the case was never solved, employees suggested a variety of suspects, from patients to hospital visitors, to janitors, and to hospital personnel. Cash had interviewed Bowen at length back then. This morning, Cash met with him. Bowen mentioned Cullum coming in late that night with a wound. A few employees whispered about the incident, but no one heard what had happened. He disappeared into his dad's office and came out an hour or so later. No one knew if anyone was in the office with him. It's suspicious Cullum was shot and Dr. Bourg claimed Tilda had embezzled. We need to find out about the missing money and if it was fraud."

"Let me call my lieutenant. If Cullum got treated, that should be enough for a search warrant."

Hawk appeared in the doorway. "Tilda Pennington had a boyfriend the weeks leading up to her death. Randy Jacobson drove a maroon Miata and he's been married twice. The last wife filed a restraining order against him."

"Let me call my lieutenant. Hawk, can you go see Randy?"

"Sure."

After she put in her call and her supervisor agreed to make the request, Sawyer stared at her. "What are you hoping to find in his files?"

"I don't know. Anything. Cullum has a stealing problem, and it's too convenient to be a coincidence for it not to be connected to the embezzlement claim Dr. Bourg had about Tilda. We should know something shortly."

The rest of the morning flew by before they heard back from the judge. The search warrants was granted. She still hadn't heard back from Hawk on Randy but hopefully would soon.

Chief Trevett agreed to have local officers help serve the warrants of Bourg's and Cullum's offices. Even though Sawyer was in security, he was not allowed to serve a warrant. Keeping to their agreement, and not wanting her to be alone, he rode to Cullum's office with her. After much going back and forth, they decided to leave Maverick at the ranch with Nora and the others. Sherriff Copeland had assigned a deputy to remain at the ranch, so it was difficult to justify taking him with them, but it was also tough to leave him behind after him being kidnapped.

Two other officers from Cedar Hollow were serving a warrant at Dr, Bourg's clinic. It was better to hit both locations at the same time, so they didn't tip off Cullum or the doctor.

As she sat in the parking lot of the clinic, butterflies danced in her stomach at the prospect of finding evidence of who killed the three people years ago.

"You look nervous," Sawyer said.

"Not nervous, anticipation is more like it." She rubbed the palm of her hands on her jeans. "There's a lot riding on this search. I've been going over everything in my head. Possible outcomes and roadblocks. Also wondering if I should've concentrated on Randy Jacobson before now."

"Being attacked forces you to speed up your investigation. Hawk is talking to Jacobson. Keep your mind on this search. The truth will come out. Do you believe Cullum will give you trouble?"

"Possibly. Especially if he's guilty. I don't see him becoming violent, but maybe he will try to use his power as the son of his doctor daddy to get me thrown out. You and I both know that's not going to happen." She added the last part for a reminder to herself. It could be intimidating when people in their own circles were powerful. She remembered once investigating the owner of a small investment company. He bowed up and started yelling how he was going to have her arrested, that he'd call the mayor in Amarillo because they were close buddies. In a matter of minutes, Mallory had him arrested, and a month later he was found guilty of embezzling money from investors.

"Is that your man?"

She glanced out the passenger window at the young officer getting out of his cruiser. "That's him, Officer Curtis Duran. I wish Ranger Barnett was here already. He's en route and should be here in a couple of hours."

"I don't blame you. I'm going to wait in the lobby. If you need anything, let me know."

"I'll do it." She got out and greeted Officer Duran. The man looked to be in his late twenties. That was the thing about small-town departments. Normally there were high turnover rates due to lower pay, but it was easier for officers to be hired fresh out of the academy. She was grateful that Duran had several years of experience.

He gave her a head nod as a greeting before they walked into the building. She turned to see Sawyer headed toward the entrance. It was unnecessary for Sawyer to be here, and she felt a little silly about not asking him to remain at the ranch. She'd never been in a situation, though, where it felt necessary to keep her son guarded but was more comfortable with him being at the ranch than here. As she walked down the hall, a middle-aged couple glanced up at her, and their gaze fixed on her badge. For some reason, it still surprised people to see a female Texas Ranger.

When they made it to Cullum's office door, she took a deep breath and walked in.

The room was small with a counter in front of her. File cabinets were neatly stacked along the wall. This might not take as long as she feared, since everything appeared to be organized.

A lady came out of a back room. "I thought I heard someone come in." Her gaze went to the badge and then to the officer behind her. "Is there something I can help you with?"

Mallory held out the warrant. "I have a warrant to search these premises."

"Uh, I don't… Mr. Bourg is not here." Nervousness danced in her eyes. "Maybe you should come back later."

She shook her head. Her heart went out the young woman

who couldn't be over twenty. It was possible she'd been hired because of her cute looks rather than her experience, but hopefully not. "It doesn't work that way. We'll need access to all the hard copy files and electronic."

Duran said, "You can remain in your office unless we need you."

Mallory jerked her head as she turned to look at him and frowned. She didn't appreciate him intervening, but she was ready to dig into the files, so she let it go.

The woman said, "Is there anything you need?"

"Are the file cabinets unlocked?" Mallory glanced around the room to see if there was anything more she wanted the receptionist to assist with.

"No. Let me go find the key."

When the woman disappeared into the back room, Officer Duran stepped up to Mallory, the hard metal of a gun barrel pressed into her side. "Don't make a sound." His voice was gruff, and his lips were close to her ear. "Put your weapon on top of the counter. If you cause trouble, a sniper will shoot the cowboy. I'm not playing games."

Out of her peripheral vision through the glass door, she could see Sawyer sitting in the lobby beside an older woman. Carefully, she slid her gun from the holster at her waist and placed it on the counter like he'd instructed. "Okay."

"We're going to walk through the lobby to my vehicle. I will be behind you. Don't try anything. I've never had a child killed—" he shrugged "—but after the cowboy gets it, I can call a hit for your boy. There's a first time for everything."

The man was insane. How had a man like this graduated from the police academy and made it through all the background checks? "I will do as you say."

"Good girl."

Irritation clawed at her for his condescending comment. Not wanting the receptionist to walk in on them, Mallory didn't waste time and stepped out of the office. She glanced across the room at Sawyer and smiled. "I need some papers from the police department. I'll meet you back here when I'm finished."

Sawyer merely nodded.

"I'll catch you later," she said.

She swallowed hard as she made it out the front door, and they made their way toward Duran's cruiser.

"Very nice. You surprise me, Ranger. I would've figured you for the hero type. I guess most females would do anything to keep their boyfriend safe. Even Rangers. Huh?" He chuckled.

She didn't respond to his taunt as she climbed in on the passenger side. As they pulled out of the parking lot, she could see Sawyer through the window, still sitting on the lobby's sofa. Her heart sank. She would've thought Sawyer would catch on to her comment. But she guessed she would have to find a way to get out of this situation without his help.

Sawyer waited for the cruiser to pull out on the road before he hurried for the door. Something was wrong, but he didn't want to put Mallory in danger. They had agreed to stay together no matter what, and he realized she was saying she'd catch him later was a code for letting him know she was in danger.

As he waited for the cruiser to leave the parking lot, he dialed Hawk's number.

"What's going on?"

"Mallory just left the clinic with Officer Duran." Sawyer pulled out and turned on the highway, careful to stay out of sight.

"You think she's in trouble?"

"Yeah. We'd agreed to stay together no matter what. She told me she was leaving with Duran to get some papers from the police department and that she'd see me later. I am following them."

"I have your location on my app. Cash and I are on our way."

"Will you make sure Maverick is okay before you leave?"

Hawk replied, "You got it."

Sawyer continued to stay back from Duran's cruiser so the man wouldn't see him. "How did it go with Randy?"

"The guy's a jerk. He served six months in jail for assault and battery of his second wife. He denied having been at Tilda's the night she was killed but claimed he was fishing at Lake Texoma. He gave me two names to back his alibi. Randy is bald and skinny as a rail. By the description of the men who attacked Mallory, Randy is not one of them. Depending on what we learn on Cullum, I'll check him out more later."

"Okay."

"Be careful, Sawyer."

No doubt, the officer threatened Mallory for her to agree to go with him. As they headed out of town, he was careful to stay even farther behind.

When the cruiser turned off the highway, he knew where they were going. Even though he wasn't familiar with this part of the county, he recognized the paved road as the address he saw for Cullum Bourg's residence.

His chest tightened. Duran was a dirty cop. Nothing disgusted Sawyer more than someone who pretended to be on the side of justice and used their position to do wrong. Did

Mallory know the trouble she was in? He had to believe she did, but he also knew she was a smart officer.

He didn't know what Cullum and Duran had planned, but he intended to do everything in his power to protect Mallory. His blood pressure rose at the thought of what he'd do if he lost her again. And this time, their little boy depended on him to safeguard his mama.

FOURTEEN

Mallory's backup service weapon remained in her ankle holster. It was comforting to know she had a way to protect herself if she could get to it without getting shot first. Her plan for the moment was to see if it was Cullum behind the murders or someone else. Officer Duran's involvement had been a surprise.

Corrupt cops always made life harder on the honest ones.

The officer pulled down the long concrete driveway of Cullum's home. There was no way anyone could afford a property like this on a lab technician's salary. It aggravated her they hadn't done a deep dive into Cullum's background to notice this earlier. Of course, they'd been preoccupied with other suspects. The kidnapping of Maverick had made the risks all too real to move about freely. That had probably been the smartest move by the suspects to stymie the investigation.

As Duran pulled behind the back of the luxurious house, her eyes lit on the red GMC Sierra. She didn't take the chance to glance back to see if Sawyer had understood her meaning. She prayed he didn't rush in to save her. Unless she needed him…

"Get out." Duran pointed his weapon at her. "Don't try

anything. I'd like nothing more than to take out a smug Ranger."

She didn't understand his rage, but she believed his words and did as he commanded.

Security cameras hung at the corner of the eaves, and they walked over a flagstone patio to the back door. He stepped around her and entered a code on the lock.

After he shoved the door open, she walked inside the house.

"Keep going." He poked her in the back with the gun.

She learned a long time ago how to take down someone behind you in training, but she was leery since Duran probably knew the same moves. She didn't want to try them just yet. There was a spacious living area with a massive stone fireplace. A mixture of thick doors, ornate crown molding and stone walls decorated the home. The overly heavy look wasn't her taste, but it would cost a pretty penny to build.

"To the right."

A bedroom stood in the middle of the wide hallway. She'd supposed they were going inside and started to enter, but Duran commanded, "Keep going."

She came to the end of the hall and stood at the stone wall. Now what?

"Step back."

After she moved, Duran reached high on the wall and pushed on a mortar joint. The wall opened to expose a hidden stairwell.

"Didn't expect that, did you?" His voice came out with a slight chuckle.

Grudgingly, she admitted to herself the door was well masked. Quickly, she retrieved a gum wrapper from her pocket and dropped it on the floor before she descended the stairs. Cullum and another man that she recognized as the man who'd tried to kidnap Maverick on her first night in Cedar Hollow stood at a wooden bar in the middle of the room. The man wore a gaudy black ring on his little finger and had cropped hair. A safe was pushed against the far wall. Two glasses of what appeared to be beer sat in front of a stool. Were they enjoying themselves waiting for her to arrive to kill her?

Chills went down her spine.

Duran had a weapon, and no doubt Cullum and the other man did, too. Besides the door she had just entered, she didn't see another exit.

"You should've stopped investigating." Cullum walked across the room and stopped in front of her. Gently he touched her cheek with the back of his hand. "It's a shame, too. You're a pretty lady."

Bile rose in her throat. Never had anyone disgusted her more. "You will be brought down."

His mouth quirked at the corner. "No one will ever find your body. As much as I'd love to play the little game of explaining what's going to happen to you, Cantrell and your boy, I simply don't have the luxury of that much time."

Pinkie man grinned like he was enjoying Cullum taunting her.

Duran said, "Get on with it. I don't want to be here any longer than necessary."

"Chill, Officer," Cullum said the last word with emphasis.

Mallory took a step to the right, toward the stairs. If she could take out at least one of them, she'd have a chance of escape, and now she knew who the players were.

A noise sounded behind her, and Mallory turned to see Dr. Bourg hurrying down the stairs.

The doctor said, "This is enough, son. Let the Ranger go."

Cullum shook his head. "I can't. You should know that. Do you want to go to prison?"

"It's gone too far. Murdering people is wrong." The doctor glanced from Cullum to the other man. And then to Duran. "What are you doing here? Are you a part of all this?" He turned back to his son. "I won't let you do it."

Duran said, "I understand your sentiment, but it's too late for that. I sure don't plan on going to prison. No one in this room better talk."

Pinkie man put his hands in the air. "I have a wife and a baby at home. I have no intentions of talking. What happens at Cullum's, stays at Cullum's." He chuckled at his own joke.

"You better not, Quinton," Cullum warned.

Mallory had just about everything she needed to bring all three men in. The name Quinton didn't ring familiar, but she would learn more soon enough. Now if she could find a way to get out of here alive and do her job.

"What about Cantrell?" the doctor asked. "You planning on killing him, too? He has a large family, and they'll never stop investigating."

"Sawyer's nothing." Cullum tossed his hand in front of him, waving away any concern.

Her chest tightened at the easy dismissal of Sawyer's life. It hurt her more than she believed possible to think of not having him around. Maverick, too. She intended to make certain that didn't happen. The stakes were high for how she handled the next few seconds. Dr. Bourg was the largest man among the four, but he was also the only one not armed, and he appeared to be having second thoughts about their attacks. She eased closer to the man.

She wasn't about to go down without a fight. The man she loved and her son depended on her.

* * *

Sawyer had heard the muffled voices from the first floor, but it had taken him a minute to notice the gum wrapper, which had to be Mallory's, and then to find the camouflaged button in the stone wall. Carefully, he made his way silently down the steps with his gun in his hand. On the third step, he paused to survey the room. Cullum and a man he recognized as Quinton Moon stood on the other side of a bar and Dr. Bourg was beside Mallory.

Mallory looked intense as she eased toward the doctor. She was outnumbered, but somehow, she still looked to be in control. His heart swelled with pride.

"That's far enough," Cullum said as he pointed at Mallory. He turned back to the doctor. "Dad, you need to go if you don't want to be a witness."

"I won't let you do it, son."

Mallory took the opportunity to throw her hip into Dr. Bourg's leg and grabbed his left arm, putting him into a submission hold from behind. If anyone tried to shoot her, the doctor would be in the line of fire.

Sawyer hurried down the remaining steps and into the room with his gun aimed at Cullum. "Drop your weapon."

Cullum didn't hesitate to fire his gun, the shot going wide of Mallory. He ran out of another door disguised as a bookshelf.

Dr. Bourg clutched his chest and slumped to the ground. A scarlet circle bloomed across his shirt. His glassy eyes stared at Mallory. "Sam didn't kill those people. I'm… I'm sorry." His face wrinkled into a frown.

Quinton tried to follow Cullum, but Sawyer commanded, "Stop, Quinton."

The man looked over his shoulder, his eyes wide, but he continued to try to squeeze past the bar and out the door.

Sawyer repeated, "Stop!"

"I got him." Mallory hurried forward, grabbing Quinton by the wrist and initiating a straight arm takedown. The move forced him to his knees, and she demanded, "Quit fighting. You are under arrest." Then she looked back to Sawyer and yelled, "Watch out."

He looked up just in time to see a man in a deputy's uniform emerge from behind the bar.

Instead of going for Sawyer, though, Officer Duran leaped over the doctor and grabbed Mallory around the waist. With two against one, Quinton freed himself and struggled to his feet.

Duran's gun pointed into her back. "Drop your weapon, Cantrell."

"You can't get away." Sawyer kept his gun in position, but the officer stayed behind Mallory. "Give up now."

Duran urged Mallory across the floor to the open hidden door. "You're in no position to make demands. Drop it or the pretty Ranger gets it in the back."

Mallory blinked rapidly, and her back stiffened as if she was waiting for the gun to blast.

The crooked officer licked his lips and smiled confidently, his eyes glistening.

Sawyer believed he'd love to shoot her and the man had nothing to lose. Sawyer dropped his weapon and put his hands in the air. "Okay."

"Don't try to be a hero, cowboy. Kick it across the floor." Duran nodded toward the wall.

Sawyer did as he asked.

"Thanks." Duran grinned. His finger tightened on the trigger as he shot Quinton at close range. "I hate weak people." Then he turned his weapon back at Sawyer.

Sawyer dove to the floor toward his own gun as another shot blasted.

Mallory screamed, "No!"

Pain lit up his shoulder as Sawyer watched Mallory lean back into Duran's grasp as she was shoved out the door.

Quinton writhed on the floor, and Dr. Bourg wasn't moving at all.

Sawyer waited for Mallory and Duran to disappear out the door before he reached for his weapon. Agony pulsed through his body and blood soaked through his sleeve, but he had to help Mallory. He clutched his weapon and climbed to his feet. Shoving the pain aside, he staggered toward the opening. He glanced out to make certain he didn't walk into gunfire from Duran or Cullum. There was no one in sight.

Where had Duran taken Mallory? Surely, they had not gotten away that quickly.

He moved along the side of the house, keeping alert for movement. As he neared the corner, someone yelled, "Watch out!"

For a second, he glanced to make certain someone hadn't yelled the warning at him, but there was no one. When he peered around the corner, he saw Cullum sitting on the ground near a fountain, his feet and hands tied with a zip tie. Confusion slammed into Sawyer. What happened?

Sawyer's gaze landed on Hawk's black truck, and relief flooded him. The cavalry had arrived.

Cullum called out while looking toward the front yard, "Kill her!"

Sawyer dashed around the house. He saw the back of Duran, who was still behind Mallory. Suddenly, Duran shoved Mallory, making her fall, and then he took off for the closest vehicle. In a quick flash, Cash flew out from behind Hawk's truck and tackled the officer to the ground.

Sawyer joined his brother and Mallory as they subdued the officer.

Hawk appeared beside them and quickly zip-tied the officer's hands behind him.

"Let me go! You're going to do time for assaulting a police officer!"

Never in his life had he been so glad to see his brothers.

Sirens sounded in the distance as Chief Trevett sped down the driveway, stopping a few feet from them. The chief climbed out of his truck and hurried over to Officer Duran, who was still whining. "Duran, stop your complaining while I talk with Cash."

Sawyer made his way to Mallory. "Are you alright?"

She nodded. "I'm not injured. But Sawyer—" she gaped "—you're bleeding."

"I'll be alright now that I know you're safe."

Her hand went to his other shoulder. "You need to go to the hospital."

His chest tightened at how close he'd come to losing her for good. Her face was still pale from the encounter, and she looked bedraggled. "I don't want to lose you again."

His words came out craggily. To his surprise, he'd never meant the words more.

FIFTEEN

Mallory turned from Sawyer and looked on as Cullum, Officer Duran and Quinton were lined up on the stone pathway in handcuffs, while Chief Trevett and his officers tried to sort out what happened. Hawk and Cash were busy speaking with the chief while the two paramedics came over and checked out Quinton.

Her mind, though, kept replaying what Sawyer had said. *I don't want to lose you again.* He must've been truly worried about her safety. She could've almost believed he wanted something more, but she didn't want to read too much into it.

"Quinton Moon, I'm surprised after our last run-in you didn't learn your lesson. This is not going to go well for you."

The younger man shook his head vehemently at the chief. "Oh no. I didn't kill nobody."

Even as the paramedic kneeled beside Quinton, the chief held out his hand. "Hold on, Moon. Let me read you your Miranda rights before you get to talking."

Cullum shouted, "Shut up, Quinton." His voice was high-pitched as he issued the threat. "They don't have anything on us. This was all of Sam Foster's doing."

Quinton wasn't even looking Cullum's way, but his complexion was pale as he looked up at the chief. Mallory knew in that moment Quinton wouldn't want to take the rap for Cullum and Duran's crimes.

The paramedic turned to the chief. "We need to get this man to the hospital."

The chief nodded. "I'll send one of my officers to follow."

A red Ford F-150 pulled up the drive and came to a stop beside the chief's Tahoe. Texas Ranger Sean Barnett. She'd almost forgotten he was supposed to assist her in the case. He got out of his truck and looked around until his gaze fell on her.

She smiled at him.

He nodded and then walked over to the chief and appeared to be listening to what was being said.

"Mom!" She turned to see Maverick running across the lawn toward her. She hurried his way, and he buried his face into her embrace. She glanced at Nora.

"Hawk let me know the bad guys were contained," Sawyer's mom quickly explained.

"Thank you for keeping him safe. I need to tell you that Maverick is your grandson."

Sawyer moved beside her.

A smile spread across the woman's lips, and her eyes twinkled as she looked at them. "I realized that the first time I met him."

"But how?"

"He looks exactly like Sawyer did at that age. I didn't know why you chose not to tell us, but I figured you had your reasons and would tell us when you were ready."

A knot of guilt formed in her stomach "I'm not fully certain I know myself, but I'd like for you and the whole

Cantrell bunch to be a part of his life." She glanced over at Sawyer, and their eyes met.

Nora held her arms out for a hug, and Mallory stepped into it. Out of the corner of her eye, she noticed Maverick staring up at them. She laughed and leaned over. "Son, this is your grandma."

"My grandma?" he said in awe. "I didn't know I had a grandma."

His words struck Mallory like a dagger to the heart. Mallory's own mother had died, so Nora was the only grandma he could know. She intended to do everything she could to make certain Maverick grew up knowing his extended family.

"I'd like to talk to you." Sawyer didn't seem to care he was interrupting a moment.

Nora held out her hand to Maverick. "Come on. Let's go look at the geese." She pointed to a nearby pond on Cullum's property.

After they had stepped away, he said, "I came too close to losing you. I don't want that to happen again."

She held up her hand, stopping him. "Please don't do this. I have no plans of staying away from Cedar Hollow or keeping Maverick out of your life. It will be tough on me when he's here for his visits, but it's for the best. I can see that. He's missed so much in his short life without getting to spend time with you and your family. But I will adjust."

He cocked his head at her and smiled. "You're always talking. If you'd listen to me…"

"Hey. I was trying to be nice." She only pretended to be offended. "I was hurt about the whole Sam thing when I thought you didn't support me. I don't blame you anymore for the police closing the case. Everyone thought Sam was guilty. It's been laid to rest now. I was hurt and even more so when I reached out after I moved to Amarillo and you didn't…"

"Mallory…"

"Let me get this out. I should've returned. I didn't want to run into Sam's accusers. I thought I could start a new life and outrun everything that had happened—"

Her words were smothered when his lips pressed against hers. It took a second to come to her senses, and she pulled away. "You're not going to distract me."

"I was talking first." He kissed her again.

For a fraction of a second her mind wrestled with telling him she had been the one who'd started the conversation, but her brain could argue with that later. She melted into his arms, and her heart lifted, feeling like everything was right.

SIXTEEN

One week later, Mallory's new bag was packed with the few things she'd bought while in Cedar Hollow. She drew a deep breath as she descended the stairs. Sadness filled her as she prepared to leave for Amarillo. For the first time since she'd moved, the West Texas town felt like anything but home.

The thought of returning to her two-bedroom house on the outskirts of town with the small fenced backyard seemed anything but peaceful. The beautiful piney woods and the wide-open spaces of the ranch seemed more welcoming.

Sawyer had taken Maverick with him to replace the living room window in her farmhouse. When she'd called her dad to tell him about Cullum and Dr. Bourg's killing of the three people, he told her he was happy she'd cleared Sam's name. It's not that Mallory didn't believe him, but he soon turned the conversation to his wife, Laura, who had gotten him a new job in IT at a local logistics company that trucked products across the United States. It was an eight-to-five job where he was home every night.

Realization of why she felt alone in trying to clear Sam's name hit her hard. Her mom was gone. Her dad had moved on. The responsibility to prove her brother's innocence and put the real killers behind bars had rested solely on her shoulders. She tried hard not to feel betrayed to have been left alone to fight for her family. Sawyer was not at fault for her family's lack of commitment.

Work required her to be back on Monday, but she had agreed to let Maverick remain at Thunder Ridge Ranch for one more week, and Sawyer would bring him to Amarillo next weekend.

Everything had worked out. Officer Duran and Cullum were both denied bail and presently sat in the county jail awaiting their trials for murder and attempted murder. Dr. Bourg hadn't survived the shooting. Quinton Moon had been released from the hospital three days after Cullum shot him. He was being brought up on charges for his involvement, but his lawyer had been able to get him out on bail. The body of Chad Kline—the man killed by the pigs—was found by police in a ravine outside of Wyndam County, less than six miles from the camping site after Quinton told him where he had disposed of him. Chad had been a longtime friend of Quinton, and Cullum had told him to get rid of the body so police wouldn't find the connection to the rest of them.

During the interrogation, Quinton told investigators that Dr. Bourg and Cullum had gone to confront Tilda at her house to persuade her to not tell investigators Dr. Bourg and his son had been committing insurance fraud. They demanded she tell them it had been her accounting mistake, but she stood behind her principles and wouldn't be persuaded to lie. In a fit of anger, Cullum grabbed her, and when she tried to defend herself, she fell and hit her head. Unknown to the doctor and son, Tilda's brother, Phillip, and Wilson Newport heard the commotion and came out of a back room where they had been working on a computer.

Phillip was armed and shot Cullum in the arm before Cullum returned fire and shot both Phillip and Wilson. Bourg and his son had loaded up the three victims in the trunk of Tilda's Malibu with the intent to drive them into the ravine of Dead Man's Curve. Before their plan could be carried out, Sam interrupted them by ramming his truck into the tree when he tried to avoid hitting her car. With Sam being unconscious, they put Tilda's jewelry and the murder weapon into his console and the bodies in his back seat. Then they pushed his truck into the ravine and drove Tilda's car back to her house and put in the garage. Investigators were still piecing together the evidence to verify the story and now had enough to prosecute Cullum before a jury.

When investigators looked into Dr. Bourg's files, they found several cases of potential insurance fraud. Everything was still preliminary, but it appeared that Bourg had been milking the insurance companies for many years, and it didn't stop until the murders.

Even though Mallory had worked in law enforcement for years, she still couldn't understand how people could do unspeakable crimes. She would like to believe Cullum would feel remorse for killing four people, including his own father, but she just didn't know.

Janet Jacobson returned to Cedar Hollow on Monday. She admitted she learned from her son Randy that while he was doing time in the county jail, he talked to Chad Kline, who'd bragged he had the Smith and Wesson gun that was used to shoot three people. Officer Duran had been paid by Cullum to steal the weapon from the evidence room. It was believed to have been used in a previous crime that left one person dead, and Cullum didn't want it being traced back to him.

When Mallory walked outside, she placed her bag in the

back seat of Sawyer's truck. Even though he offered to drive to Amarillo, she had turned him down. Ranger Barnett remained in Cedar Hollow to help her finish her paperwork on the case, and then he took yesterday afternoon off to go fishing. She would ride back with him, where her Texas Ranger issued truck awaited at her home. Nora, Shaylee and Emma had already said their goodbyes, hugs included. Cash waved at her from the barn, and she returned the gesture.

It had taken everything in her not cry.

As she pulled up the drive to her farm, she was struck with the beauty she'd never noticed before. One hundred and sixty acres of mostly pasture and farmland. Pine and oak trees gathered in clusters that gave it the perfect mix. The two-story farmhouse was in desperate need of renovation. The roof needed replacing and the white paint was peeling. The windows needed to be switched out with energy-efficient ones. Even with that, the thought of the farm being her own brought her satisfaction and made her want to keep it.

Why did she feel like she was leaving the best part of her behind?

Melancholy weighed heavily on her, and she prayed it would go away once she returned to Amarillo. But deep in her soul, she knew things could never be as before. Maverick would be spending time with Sawyer as he should. There would be trips back and forth to Cedar Hollow and Sawyer would come to her house.

When she walked up the porch, she didn't hear anyone. But a large bouquet of wildflowers in a mason jar sat on the kitchen counter. She smiled at the gesture. Even in the dust-covered, mostly empty home, the bright bluebonnets and buttercups cheered up the place. "Maverick? Sawyer?"

When no one answered, she noticed Sawyer's truck was

parked on the north side of the barn, and she headed that way. As she approached, she heard Maverick giggling.

"Now, Daddy?" Her son's voice was bursting with excitement.

"Yeah," Sawyer whispered back.

"What are you two up to?" She rounded the corner, and her eyes lit on Maverick decked out in jeans, boots and a new cowboy hat. Mollie Beth stood at his side. Mallory's gaze went back to Sawyer, who held an even larger bouquet of flowers than was in the house in his left hand, since his right arm was in a sling from the gunshot wound. He simply stared at her with a big smile, and the cleft in his chin was more pronounced.

"Surprise!" Maverick shouted and held his hands in the air.

She put her hand on her hip. "Did I forget my birthday?"

Mav giggled. "No..."

"Hey, sport." Sawyer patted the top of Maverick's new hat. "Let me take it from here."

She didn't know what these two had cooked up, but she was intrigued, even though she needed to get on the road.

Sawyer went down to one knee and attempted to dig something from the inside of his sling. A low growl came from him as he removed the contraption. "I'm already tired of wearing this thing." He retrieved a blue velvet box.

Her heart stuttered.

"Will you marry me, Mal?"

She drew a deep breath as the blood rushed through her ears. Then she shook her head. "We've been through this before."

He cocked his head at her. "That was five years ago. I've changed. I was wrong for not helping investigate longer and digging deeper, for making you feel like I wouldn't stand by you. I never intended for that to happen. I'm not going to lie to you. I was stubborn back then and still am a mite." He climbed to his feet. "But I can promise you this, I will always…*always* stand by you." His dark eyes seemed to take her in.

"I think I've always known it, but it hurt more than it should. I was blaming you for the police's quick move to blame Sam, and even my mom's drinking that led to her death."

"Marry me, Mal. I've missed having you in my world."

"What about my job?"

"We'll work something out. I'd rather not move to Amarillo, but if it means having you beside me, I will. I'm sure I could buy a small ranch or something."

She laughed. She knew moving away from Thunder Ridge Ranch and not being here with his brothers was a huge offer. "That'd be like raising a herd of longhorns in the middle of Times Square. Not saying it couldn't be done, but maybe a little out of place." She laughed again and then lowered her voice to a whisper. "Are you certain you're not just wanting to marry me for Maverick's sake?"

"Our son means the world to me, but…" He glanced at Maverick and smiled. "I'd want you to be my wife even if we didn't have a child. I love you. Always have."

She wrapped her arms around his neck and kissed him again. "I'd be honored to be your wife. I love you, too. Last night I talked with Texas Ranger Jim Clark, the agent whose mother sits for Maverick, and he said there's an opening coming up in Company B. He agreed to put in a good word for me. One more thing—you need to listen to the doctor and wear the sling for two more weeks."

"There you go again, always having to have the last

word." He gave her another kiss on the lips. "This time I like it."

Maverick looked up at them. "Yay! Can I have a horse?"

They both laughed and answered in unison, "Yes."

EPILOGUE

Two months later...

With a storage tub filled with food, Mallory knocked the screen door open with her hip and walked down the back steps. "I hope y'all are hungry."

"We sure are," Sawyer hollered back. He climbed down a ladder from the steep roof and dropped his hammer on the ground.

She carried the lunch over to the clump of trees that provided a canopy of shade. Being it was still September, the Texas heat was still in the mid-nighties. The men had already set up tables built from of sawhorses and sheets of plyboard.

Sawyer's family had come over to the farmhouse to put on the new roof today. Four of his brothers had been here since sunup, and they hoped to have the roof completed by the end of the day.

She set the food on the makeshift table—fried chicken, mashed potatoes with cream gravy, along with a salad and cantaloupe. Nora brought the sweet tea and lemonade out, while Shaylee and Holly carried the desserts and paper goods.

It was hard to believe she and Sawyer had been married

four weeks after a quaint family wedding at the local church where his family, and now they, too, worshipped. Her dad and stepmom flew in for the ceremony. She appreciated the gesture even though they were only able to stay one night. It was a step in the right direction to mending fences.

She prayed every night Brock, the youngest Cantrell, would reach out and repair the relationship with his family. Sawyer only told her three things—his little brother had taken off, he was alive and hadn't come home even for their father's funeral. It was a proverbial spur under the saddle for the close-knit family.

Nora offered to give them a piece of Thunder Ridge Ranch, but she and Sawyer agreed to make this one-hundred-sixty acre farm/ranch their own. A few months ago, she'd never guessed this place would feel like home, but joy settled on her every time she looked out from the porch at the open land, barn, and animals.

Her application to be transferred to Company B in the Texas Ranger was approved, and she planned to start in the new field office in a week.

"Everyone wash up," Nora told them as Cash and Hawk reached for paper plates.

The brothers glanced at each other with a knowing smile before they filed into the house to do her bidding.

Sawyer strode up to her after washing. "Smells delicious."

"Thanks, but your mom and Shaylee did most of the work, and Holly baked the pies."

"Don't be so modest. I know you were busy cooking, too." He gave her a peck on the cheek.

He was right, but she felt like her culinary abilities lacked compared to the others. She had to admit spending time with them made her appreciate homecooked meals.

Maverick galloped up to the table with his plastic calf toy in tow. “Daddy, can I ride Smokey, now?”

She noticed Sawyer’s chest puff up with pride every time Maverick called him daddy.

Smokey was Maverick’s new black roan horse that looked like a darker version of Sawyer’s horse, Steel. They hadn’t allowed Maverick to ride by himself, but Sawyer led him around by the reins at least once a day.

He rubbed him on top of his sandy blond head. “That’s right. We need to eat lunch first, and us cowboys have a lot of work to do repairing the roof on our house. You don’t want it to rain on your bed, do you?”

“No,” Maverick answered wryly like that was a ridiculous question. “It can’t rain in the house.”

After Hawk said the blessing for the meal and everyone dug in to eat, she tugged Sawyer to the side of house on the wrap around porch.

She stood on her tip toes and kissed his cheek. “Thank you.”

“For what?” He cocked his head at her in question, a twinkle in his eye.

“For everything. I’ve never felt so content and peaceful in my life. Being part of the Cantrells is far more of a blessing than I ever imagined.”

“Remember that in a few months. I’ve been told we can be a little too much too handle.”

“Never.” She wrapped her arms around his neck, and their lips met. The kiss held promise of a lifetime to come.

* * * * *

If you liked this story from Connie Queen, check out her previous Love Inspired Suspense books:

Justice Undercover
Texas Christmas Revenge
Canyon Survival
Abduction Cold Case
Tracking the Tiny Target
Rescuing the Stolen Child
Wilderness Witness Survival
Searching for Justice
Shielded by the Cowboy

Available now from Love Inspired Suspense!
Find more great reads at LoveInspired.com.

Dear Reader,

Thank you for joining me on Sawyer and Mallory's journey.

I love stories about law enforcement, but being from Texas, I'm partial to the Texas Rangers. Hence why I made Mallory a Ranger. Who doesn't love law officers in boots, jeans and a Stetson?

Did you know to qualify to be a Ranger, you must have a minimum of eight years in law enforcement and be employed with the Texas Department of Public Safety? (So, no twenty-three-year-olds allowed…) The average Ranger is forty-four years old. Even though the first female Texas Rangers were hired in 1993, they are still uncommon in the department. The first female to make Texas Ranger Major was only in 2023. If you ever find yourself near Waco, stop by and visit the Texas Ranger Museum.

Texas Cowboy Protector is the second book of the Thunder Ridge Justice Series. I'm currently working on the next book in the series.

I love to hear from readers. You can connect with me on my Facebook page at www.facebook.com/queenofheartthrobbingsuspense, or keep up with my latest news and books on my website at www.conniequeenauthor.com.

Connie Queen